The Cat of Christmas Present

by

Kathi Daley

This book is a work of fiction. Names, characters, places, and incidents either are products of the author's imagination or are used fictitiously. Any resemblance to actual events or locales or persons, living or dead, is entirely coincidental.

I want to thank the very talented Jessica Fischer for the cover art.

I so appreciate Bruce Curran, who is always ready and willing to answer my cyber questions, and Peggy Hyndman for helping sleuth out those pesky typos.

And, of course, thanks to the readers and bloggers in my life, who make doing what I do possible.

Thank you to Randy Ladenheim-Gil for the editing.

Special thanks to Nancy Farris, Joanne Kocourek, Elizabeth Dent, Lisa Millett, Pam Curran, Karen Owen, Linda Mierka, and Marie Rice for submitting recipes.

And finally I want to thank my sister Christy for always lending an ear and my husband Ken for allowing me time to write by taking care of everything else.

Books by Kathi Daley

Come for the murder, stay
for the romance.

Zoe Donovan Cozy Mystery:

Halloween Hijinks
The Trouble With Turkeys
Christmas Crazy
Cupid's Curse
Big Bunny Bump-off
Beach Blanket Barbie
Maui Madness
Derby Divas
Haunted Hamlet
Turkeys, Tuxes, and Tabbies
Christmas Cozy
Alaskan Alliance
Matrimony Meltdown
Soul Surrender
Heavenly Honeymoon
Hopscotch Homicide
Ghostly Graveyard
Santa Sleuth
Shamrock Shenanigans
Kitten Kaboodle
Costume Catastrophe
Candy Cane Caper
Holiday Hangover – *January 2017*

Zimmerman Academy The New Normal

Ashton Falls Cozy Cookbook

Tj Jensen Paradise Lake Mysteries by Henery Press

Pumpkins in Paradise
Snowmen in Paradise
Bikinis in Paradise
Christmas in Paradise
Puppies in Paradise
Halloween in Paradise
Treasure in Paradise – *April 2017*

Whales and Tails Cozy Mystery:

Romeow and Juliet
The Mad Catter
Grimm's Furry Tail
Much Ado About Felines
Legend of Tabby Hollow
The Cat of Christmas Past
A Tale of Two Tabbies
The Great Catsby
Count Catula
The Cat of Christmas Present

Winters Tail

Future

Seacliff High Mystery:
The Secret
The Curse
The Relic
The Conspiracy
The Grudge

Sand and Sea Hawaiian Mystery:
Murder at Dolphin Bay
Murder at Sunrise Beach
Murder at the Witching Hour
Murder at Christmas – *December 2016*

Road to Christmas Romance:
Road to Christmas Past

Chapter 1

Monday, December 12

The day Clarence came into my life started off like any other. I woke as the stars in the night sky faded into the early dawn, pulled on a pair of heavy sweats, and headed downstairs to toss a log on the embers that remained from the previous night's fire. My dog Max wasn't thrilled to leave the comfort of the bed; still, he lumbered along behind me as I went about my morning routine. It was a cold and drizzly day. Max went to lay by the fire as I looked out the window and watched the angry sea crash onto the beach. I hoped the temperature would drop a few degrees so the moisture that was drenching the island would turn to snow, providing us with the white Christmas I longed for.

"So, what do you think, Max? Do we brave the elements and go for a run or do we stay inside near the fire and enjoy the colorful lights Cody helped put up?" I asked, referring to my boyfriend, Cody West.

Today was a Monday, which meant Coffee Cat Books, the coffee bar/bookstore/cat lounge I owned and operated along with my best friend, Tara O'Brian, was closed, affording me a degree of freedom in my morning routine. Max opened one eye to acknowledge that I'd spoken, but then promptly went back to sleep. Not that I blamed him. There are times in your life when wrapping yourself into a warm comforter and sipping coffee in front of a cozy fire seems to be the most important thing in the world.

I picked up the remote and turned on the stereo. I'd dug out some of my old CDs and loaded a selection of Christmas music I'd enjoyed as a child. There was something nostalgic about cuddling up by the fire, listening to the classics while a storm brewed outside. My siblings didn't really get why I loved the old carols by Bing Crosby and Frank Sinatra when modern stars had recorded newer renditions of the oldies but goodies, but I guess when it comes down to it, I'm an old soul at heart.

I have fond memories of sitting on my dad's lap, listening to the sweet voices of those who by now have passed while my mom baked cookies in the kitchen and my older siblings squabbled over the TV remote while my younger sister napped peacefully in a nearby playpen. I love my family and I love all the big, noisy holiday moments, but those special times, when it was just the two of us, will forever be burned into my heart.

Deciding to at the very least delay leaving the warmth of my cabin, I poured myself a cup of coffee and was heading back to the sofa when the phone rang.

"Good morning, Tara," I greeted her.

"I'm sorry to call so early, but I have news."

My senses jumped into high alert as I detected the catch in Tara's voice. It sounded like she'd been crying. "What's wrong? Is everyone okay?"

"Everyone is okay. It's not that."

"Then what?"

"I woke up early this morning, so I decided to deal with the pile of mail that's been cluttering my dining room table."

With the approach of the holiday, Tara and I had been really busy at the bookstore, and we'd both complained that ordinary tasks simply weren't being attended to. "And…?"

"There was a letter from the bank." Tara paused and let out a long breath. "They sold our loan."

I knew immediately that Tara was referring to the loan on the bookstore.

"Can they do that?"

"Apparently, they can."

"Okay." I took a minute to let this bit of information digest. "I guess that isn't necessarily a bad thing."

"But it is," Tara insisted. "Remember last spring when money was tight and we were two weeks late with our loan payment?"

"Yeah. I remember. But the man at the bank said he understood the seasonality of the businesses on the island and it didn't seem to be a big deal."

"And do you remember last month, when the loan payment slipped between the seats in my car and was never mailed even though I was sure I mailed it?"

"I remember. It was our second late payment, so we had to pay a late fee. You aren't still beating yourself up over that, are you? It was an accident. It could have happened to anyone."

"It didn't happen to anyone; it happened to me, and now I'm responsible for us losing the store."

At this point Tara began to sob.

"Losing the store? What are you talking about?"

I waited while Tara pulled herself together. I couldn't remember the last time she'd been this upset, but based on the sounds coming through the phone it was as if she was close to being hysterical.

"Tara?" I asked again. "Just tell me what's going on."

I heard her take several deep breaths before answering. "Apparently, there's a clause in our loan contract that states that if we're late with two payments in any twelve-month period, even by one day, the lender, if they so desire, can call in the loan, payable in full."

"Payable in full? That's crazy. We'd never sign something like that."

"Apparently we did. I guess it was part of the small print. The woman I spoke to at the bank said they never really take advantage of the due-on-demand option, especially if the payment is made right away, but our loan was sold to an investor who's executing the clause. We only have thirty days from the date of the letter to either pay the loan in full or vacate the premises."

"There's no way we can pay off the loan. There has to be something we can do. We'll call an attorney."

"We can't afford an attorney."

"So we'll call the man who owns the loan now. What's his name?"

"Anthony Princeton of Princeton Enterprises."

"Is there a number to call on the letter?"

"Yeah. There is a number, which I called, but the person who answered said Mr. Princeton was out of the office and wouldn't be back until after the holidays. I asked if there was someone else I could speak to and she said no. What are we going to do?"

I had no idea. There was no way we could pay off the loan in thirty days and Tara was right; we couldn't afford to pay an attorney to straighten things out. "I'll talk to Siobhan," I said, referring to my older sister, who happened to be a savvy businesswoman and the mayor of Madrona Island. "She's always been good at figuring out these types of things. Hang in there and I'll call you as soon as I can."

I hung up the phone, wrapped a quilt around my body, and had a good cry. The bookstore meant everything to Tara and me. We'd worked so hard and were finally beginning to make enough of a profit to maybe even start getting ahead. Thinking back, we'd been in such a rush to get the loan to open the store that we probably hadn't been as conscientious as we should have about reading the fine print. I'm sure if we knew about the due-on-demand clause we would have refused to sign the contract. Of course, neither of us planned on being late with our payments, so we might not have made a fuss about the condition even if we'd realized the clause was there.

I looked longingly around the cozy room as I came to terms with the fact that my relaxing day off was now going to be nothing more than an unrealized dream. I'd headed to the kitchen to make some breakfast before calling Siobhan when I heard a scratch at the door.

"Meow."

I looked down to find a large, beautiful, and completely soaked cat sitting on my doorstep.

"What are you doing out here?"

The cat didn't answer, instead darting inside. Based on the fact that he ran directly to Max, I was willing to bet this early morning visitor was one of my witchy friend Tansy's magical cats. Sure, my Aunt Maggie owns a cat sanctuary, and it isn't unusual for people to simply drop cats off on our doorstep, but most cats are skittish around Max until they get to know him. When I have a feline visitor who cozies up to Max without a bit of hesitation, ten times out of ten, the animal in question has been sent to me for a reason.

Max got up and began wagging his tail as he greeted this new friend. I groaned as both animals headed to the door. It wasn't a good sign that my previously mellow dog was suddenly wide awake and ready to head out into the chilly morning.

"Do you think maybe we can do this later?" I asked the cat.

"Meow."

"It's just that it's cold and drizzly this morning and this is my day off. Or it's supposed to be. Tara called with a huge problem, so now instead of a relaxing morning I need to call my sister for help. But I hoped I'd be able to get the bank thing straightened out and still have time left to watch some old Christmas movies. I think *It's a Wonderful Life* is on cable. And if I get really ambitious I thought I might start wrapping the mountain of gifts I've accumulated over the past few weeks, and maybe even bake some cookies."

The cat crossed the room and jumped up onto the counter. He knocked my phone to the floor just as it rang. I let out a sigh as I watched my lazy morning melting away. I picked up the phone and looked at the caller ID.

"Good morning, Tansy," I greeted the witch who lived in Pelican Bay with her partner, Bella.

"Good morning, Caitlin. I'm sorry to bother you so early in the morning, but I wanted to make sure Clarence had arrived safely."

"He's here and seems to want to show me something. Outside. In the cold. I don't suppose it can wait?"

"Normally I let you set the pace with the cats that are sent to you, but I have a premonition that time is of the essence now. You must go with Clarence and you mustn't delay."

I looked longingly at the cozy sofa and warm fire. "Do you know what we're looking for?"

"I don't, but Clarence does. He'll lead you to wherever you're needed. Now hurry. There's no time to waste."

I hung up and slipped a raincoat over my sweats and tennis shoes onto my feet. Then I grabbed my phone and headed toward the door, where Max and Clarence were waiting. I pulled my hood up over my head as I went out into the increasingly heavy storm. Clarence started toward the beach, which had receded considerably as the wind-fueled surf covered the sand. I put my head down and pushed forward as I struggled to make my way through the storm. Clarence was going in the direction of Mr. Parsons's property, which was located to the left of my aunt's estate. He lived in a huge mansion with Cody and Harland Jones, who had recently joined them after his home had burned to the ground. As I struggled to keep up with Max and Clarence, I prayed the magical cat wasn't leading me to some gruesome discovery involving a resident of that very house.

I'm not sure why I was chosen, by whomever or whatever, to act as a human vessel for the cats who migrated in and out of my life. All I know is that when a mystery presents itself, a cat arrives. I certainly didn't ask to be thrust into the role of amateur sleuth, nor is investigating murders something I would have chosen for myself. That being said, I'm also the sort who never turns her back on a person in need.

I felt a sense of relief when Clarence continued on down the beach when he arrived at the path leading from the beach to Mr. Parsons's home. Every single person living in that mausoleum of a house is special to me, so I'd found myself almost unable to breathe as Clarence had trotted in that direction.

The wind seemed to increase in strength as each moment passed, and by the time Clarence stopped, at what I assumed was our destination, I was almost out of breath. Struggling against the wind and rain for almost thirty minutes is exhausting even for someone like me, who's in pretty good shape. At first I didn't understand why Clarence had led me to this isolated location. Mr. Parsons's house was behind me and the home of a hippie couple who lived down the beach was just ahead of me. I looked around, but it didn't seem as if there was anything to find other than a whole lot of sand and water.

"Okay. I'm here. What am I looking for?"

Clarence headed to a large rock just above the waterline, while Max ran around in a circle, barking.

I joined him at the rock, terrified of what I might find. As I've indicated before, generally speaking, when one of Tansy's magical cats comes to me, someone has died and the cat has been sent to help me find the killer.

When I rounded the corner to find a body on the other side of the rock, I knew I was right in my assumption. I knelt down to take a closer look at the man, who seemed as if he might be asleep rather than dead. I gently placed two fingers on his neck to feel for a pulse just as he suddenly opened his eyes.

I hate to confess this, but I, Caitlin Hart, screamed like a girl. Okay, I know I *am* a girl, but I like to think I've evolved to the point where I no longer scream like one at every dead body that crosses my path.

I watched the man as he put his hand to his forehead, which was covered with blood. "Where am I? Who are you?"

"My name is Cait. I live down the beach." I nodded toward the animals. "Max and Clarence found you. I thought you were dead."

He groaned.

"Don't worry. I'll call for help."

I took my phone out of my pocket and dialed Ryan Finnegan, the resident deputy and my almost brother-in-law. Once I'd told him what was going on he told me to sit tight and promised he was on his way.

"Help is on the way. Are you okay? Can I do something?"

The man opened his mouth as if to speak and then closed his eyes. I was afraid I'd lose him before help arrived. I shook his arm and gently guided him back into consciousness. "What's your name?" I asked.

"Name?"

"What do people call you?"

The man looked confused.

I pointed to myself. "My name is Caitlin Hart, but everyone calls me Cait. And you are...?"

A pained look came over his face.

"It's okay; we can figure that out later. Please just try to stay awake. Finn didn't say so specifically, but I'm pretty sure that's the right thing to do."

He tried to sit up, but before he made it even halfway he fell back onto the sand.

"Just lay still. I think I hear the sirens now."

I didn't hear them yet, but I wanted to give him something to cling to.

"So, do you live on the island?" I asked conversationally.

He didn't answer, but I could see by the look on his face he wasn't sure what I was asking.

"I guess asking for answers is a lot, given the trauma to your head, so how about I tell you about me?"

He closed his eyes again, but I could see he was still breathing and he moved his arm slightly.

"Like I said, my name is Cait. We're on Madrona Island. I thought you might want to know that if you're feeling confused. I was born here and I've lived here my entire life. I love this island. It's like a part of the family. I doubt I'll ever leave." I knew I was rambling, but at that moment rambling was the only thing I could come up with.

The man groaned.

"Are you okay?"

"Dizzy."

"Just lie still. It won't be long now." I laced the fingers on his right hand through mine so he would know he wasn't alone and gave the hand a gentle squeeze, hoping to comfort him. He gently squeezed my hand in return. "I have two brothers and two sisters," I continued. "My oldest brother, Aiden, is a fisherman, but he's home for the winter. He lives in Harthaven, and so do my mother and youngest sister."

I glanced at him and thought he looked to be closer to death than he was when I arrived. "Are you still with me?"

He didn't answer but squeezed my hand just a bit tighter.

"My next older brother is Danny. He lives on a boat in the marina at Pelican Bay. He runs fishing and whale watch tours, but I'm sure he isn't operating on a day like today." I took a deep breath and prayed the man, whose skin had taken on a bluish-gray tint, wouldn't die before Finn arrived. "My older sister, Siobhan, is the mayor. She lived in Seattle for a while but then moved home after being fired for no good reason at all as far as I'm concerned. She isn't only the mayor; she's also engaged to the resident deputy, who I'm sure will be here any minute."

I reached out with my free hand and touched him on the arm. He moved just a bit.

Rain had drenched my clothing and was running off the hood of my raincoat but I continued to ramble on. I mean really, what else was there to do? I doubted he was taking in a word I was saying, but it made me feel better to keep talking. "And then there's Cassidy, Cassie for short. She's a teenager and a real handful. She lives in Harthaven with my mother. They used to share the family home, but it burned down last summer, so now they live in a condo. I think Mom likes the condo okay. It's certainly less upkeep than the house was, which not only sat on a huge lot but had six bedrooms. But Cassie...Cassie seems lost since the fire. I do feel for her. All her belongings were destroyed, and I think that's left her feeling like she's afloat in the sea without a life raft."

The man's eyes flickered open, then closed again. I realized I needed to say something interesting enough to keep him awake. I tried to think of something, but the only thing I could come up with was shocking.

"My aunt is engaged to a priest."

I guess shocking worked; he opened one eye and looked at me.

"It's unofficial, and no one other than me and Siobhan knows. As you can imagine, it's a huge secret. I'm not supposed to tell anyone, but it's hard keeping it from everyone."

"I must be dying." The man groaned.

"What? No. Why would you think that?" I bluffed. He really did look like he was knocking on death's door.

"You told me your secret. You wouldn't have done that if you didn't think I wouldn't be around to tell someone else."

Good going, Cait. Way to comfort the guy. "I'm sure you're not dying. In fact, you're looking much better," I lied. "I just figured you wouldn't remember this conversation, so it was okay to tell you. But if you do remember it, you can't tell anyone."

He didn't answer.

"Swear to me you'll keep my secret."

The man smiled a tiny little half smile. Despite the fact that he was half dead, it almost seemed like he was teasing me with his crooked smile and lack of reply. I noticed that if you looked beyond the bluish-gray tint of his skin and the huge gash on his forehead, he was a handsome man.

"Are you still with me?"

He closed his eyes again and didn't answer. I was pretty sure he'd died, but in the event he was just resting his eyes, I added, "Finn, short for Ryan Finnegan, is a great guy. I'm sure he's almost here. I know I've said that a bunch of times before, but this time I really mean it. Please hang on. I promise you he'll take good care of you." It appeared as if he was no longer breathing. "Just a little longer." I used my free hand to lift one of his eyelids. Blue. The man had the most amazing blue eyes. "Please don't die."

When Finn and the local paramedic arrived on the scene I filled them in on what I knew, which wasn't a lot. I couldn't help but wonder how this man had ended up half dead on an isolated beach in the middle of a storm, but I guessed I was going to have to wait for an explanation. I watched as he was loaded onto a stretcher and taken away.

Max trotted over and sat down beside me. The rain was getting harder and we'd done what we could, so I supposed it was time to head back home. I looked down at Clarence and wondered if our job was complete or if, in fact, it was just beginning.

Chapter 2

As soon as Max, Clarence, and I returned to my cabin, I dried the animals and then fed them before heading upstairs for a hot shower and dry clothes. By the time I came down, Siobhan and Cody were waiting for me. I'd called Finn at home, so it made sense my sister would know what was going on and, knowing Siobhan, it also made sense she would call Cody. The three of us, along with Tara and, sometimes, my brother Danny, had somehow become Finn's unofficial sleuthing team.

"What do we know?" my überefficient sister asked before I even had a chance to greet them.

I explained what I knew, which wasn't a lot, after I'd poured myself a cup of coffee and joined the others sitting around the kitchen table.

"So are we thinking the man came to be passed out on the beach of his own accord?" Siobhan attempted to clarify.

"Like I said, he had a gash on his head, so it appeared someone had hit him and left him for dead, but I suppose if he was drunk he might have passed out and hit his head on the rock he was lying near. I guess it's too soon to tell. Maybe Finn will be able to fill us in once the guy is checked out by a doctor. In the meantime, there isn't a lot we can do."

"You're right," Siobhan acknowledged. "I think I'll go home and get ready for work. If foul play was involved and the Scooby gang needs to assemble, just let me know."

"I will. But as long as you're here, there's something else I need to talk to you about." I explained about the letter Tara had received.

Siobhan frowned. "It's certainly possible a due-on-demand clause was written into the contract. I'll stop by Tara's on my way home to take a look at the letter. Even if there is such a clause it's reasonable we should be able to speak to the person who bought the loan. I know Tara didn't get anywhere with the receptionist, but maybe as the mayor of Madrona Island I'll have more luck. I'll call you when I know something."

Siobhan and Cody both left for work and I was once again alone on my slightly less relaxing day off. Finding a man half dead on the beach coupled with the fear that we might lose the bookstore had completely destroyed the snuggle-in-and-relax mood I'd been in earlier in the morning. Siobhan was much better equipped to deal with the bookstore situation than I, so I decided to have some breakfast and head to the hospital to find out what I could about our John Doe—the only name I had for him at the moment. I was sure he'd give the hospital all the information they needed by now, though.

Boy, was I wrong.

"What do you mean, he doesn't know who he is?" I asked Dr. Matthew Ryan when I arrived at the hospital later that day.

"He's suffered a head trauma that seems to have led to amnesia. It may wear off once he has a chance to heal a bit," the doctor in charge told me.

"And in the meantime?"

Dr. Ryan, who happened to be the father of one of my childhood friends and a parishioner at St. Patrick's Catholic Church, looked at me but didn't speak at first. "If his memory doesn't come back I'm hoping Finn can figure out who he is. He told me he was going to check missing person's reports, and if that doesn't turn up anything he's going to come by here to take a set of fingerprints. I'm sure we'll figure this whole thing out in the next couple of days."

"And if nothing works? If he doesn't remember who he is and Finn isn't able to identify him? What will happen to him then?"

"Honestly, I'm not sure. But it's too soon to worry about that. I can justify keeping him in the hospital for a couple of days, which should give us the time we need to figure this out."

I hated to think of the poor guy alone in a place he couldn't even remember. Chances were someone would report him missing.

"Did he have any personal possessions with him when he was brought in? Maybe a wallet?" I wondered.

"There was nothing in his pockets. It's possible he may have been injured during the course of a robbery."

"Can I speak to him?"

"He's been sedated. If you come by later this afternoon I can give you a few minutes with him. And Cait..."

"Yeah?"

"It will be only a few minutes."

"Okay. I'll call to check with you before I come back."

On my way out I called Finn, who told me he hadn't found a wallet or any sort of identification when John Doe had been picked up by emergency personnel. And no one matching his description had been reported missing. Of course it was early still; there was a good chance his family and friends simply didn't know he was missing yet. Before I hung up Finn promised to let me know if he found out anything more about the victim.

I decided to go back to the beach where I'd found John Doe. Perhaps he had had something in his pockets that had fallen out during his ordeal. The tide would have come in by this point, though, so any evidence that might have existed would most likely be underwater, but if there was something to find I knew Max or Clarence would be more likely than me to find it. I stopped back by my cabin and picked them both up. Luckily, the rain had stopped at least for the time being. It was still overcast and I had a feeling the reprieve might be short-lived, but because others were taking care of the loan problem, finding out exactly who John Doe was suddenly seemed like the most important task in my day.

I couldn't imagine the terror I'd feel if I woke up in a strange place without even the memory of who I was or how I had gotten there. Dr. Ryan had said John

Doe's injuries were relatively minor, but it did seem odd to me that a minor injury that would result in such a short hospital stay would result in complete and total amnesia. Not that I knew a lot about it. I'd seen a few television programs dealing with amnesia and it seemed like the loss of memory was most often the result of an act of violence, coupled with some sort of trauma the victim was unable to process.

I wondered what sort of trauma had initiated the man's forgetfulness if that was, indeed, even what had happened.

When Max, Clarence, and I arrived at the spot on the beach where we'd found John Doe that morning, it took my canine and feline sleuths all of two minutes to come up with a wallet I hoped belonged to the victim. The problem was that there was nothing inside it to lead me to the identity of the man I'd found earlier in the day. A robbery could account for the fact that credit cards, cash, or sources of identification were missing. The only thing I found in the wallet was a receipt from the Driftwood Café from Saturday, a receipt from the Christmas store in town, which was likewise dated Saturday, an order form from a florist that wasn't dated, and a key that looked like it might open a door of some type.

Because it was almost lunchtime and I never had gotten around to breakfast, I called Cody to see if he wanted to meet me at the Driftwood for a sandwich; that seemed as good a spot as any to begin my search. Luckily, he was free, so we agreed to a time and I headed back to the cabin to shower and change into clean clothes. I decided on a pair of faded jeans and a bright red sweater with a Christmassy feel. There were times I found it difficult to juggle all the obligations in my life and seemed to completely miss out on the magic of a season, but this year, despite the new mystery that had landed in my lap and my worry about the store, I was bound and determined to eke out every bit of Christmas spirit the holiday had to offer.

I made sure Max and Clarence were happy, fed, and settled in for a few hours, then headed into town.

"Love the light-up earrings," Cody complimented after he kissed me hello.

I touched one of the bulbs that hung from my ear. "Thanks. I've had these for years, but I haven't worn them since I was a teenager. I decided a little holiday overindulgence was in order."

"I totally agree, and I'm looking forward to overindulging with you. Maybe we can talk about making some plans for the next couple of weeks once we help your John Doe sort things out."

"I'd love that. I guess we should get a table. It's getting crowded already."

"I've already requested a booth in the back so we can chat while we eat."

"Great. Just give me a minute to ask the new girl working at the register if she remembers seeing John Doe on Saturday. If the waitress comes by order me a turkey club and a soda."

"Fries or onion rings?"

"Onion rings. And no mayonnaise on the sandwich."

"Got it." Cody headed toward the booth while I went to the cash register.

I described the man I'd found on the beach, and the fact that there were receipts for flowers and Christmas decorations in a wallet I suspected was his as well as one from the café, the cashier nodded and said she thought she knew who he was. She hadn't caught his name and he'd paid with cash, but she did remember he'd told his waitress that he was on the island for a holiday getaway with a special someone. After determining that the waitress who'd served him was on shift, I asked the cashier to have her stop by our table when she got the chance.

"The prime rib sandwich looked good, so I ordered that for myself and the turkey club for you," Cody said when I joined him. "They have cherry cheesecake for dessert, so I may have to indulge."

"Do you have a full hour or do you have to hurry back?"

"I have an interview with the chairperson for the St. Patrick's spaghetti feed at one, but I'm all yours until then. Do you have any news since this morning?"

I filled Cody in on the information I'd gotten from Dr. Ryan. Right now I was most concerned that the poor man not be shuffled off to a mental health facility before we could help him remember who he was.

"It may come back to him on its own," Cody pointed out.

"I hope so. It's less than two weeks until Christmas and I'd really love to be able to focus on family, friends, and community events. After the murder at Halloween I feel sleuthed out."

"So let's talk about something else," Cody suggested. "At least until the waitress who spoke to John Doe makes her way over to us."

"I wonder if Siobhan has gotten through to anyone at Princeton Enterprises about the status of our loan."

"Let's talk about something that isn't going to give you indigestion," Cody suggested gently.

Between the bookstore crisis and the unidentified man in the hospital, it was going to be hard to engage in idle chitchat, but I agreed with Cody; talking about either while we ate probably would give me a stomachache.

"Are we still on for tree shopping tonight?" I asked, trying for a lighter topic.

"We are. I have a list of everyone we need to buy a tree for. Francine wants a twelve-footer at least," Cody said, referring to Francine Rivers, my aunt's next-door neighbor to the right. "Mr. Parsons wants a six- to eight-foot tree for the study. Your mother said she wasn't going to get a tree this year, but Cassie was afraid she'd end up regretting it, so she wants us to get a small one, not more than six feet tall and thin, maybe a silvertip. Your Aunt Maggie requested at least a twelve-foot white fir, preferably with even branches and no bare spots. If we add in a tree for your cabin and one for my apartment, that makes six."

"It's a good thing you have a truck."

"I think having a truck is what led to the full load. Everyone I've spoken to in the past few days greeted me with 'because you have a truck, do you mind picking up a tree for me when you get yours?' I don't mind, though. We had a lot of fun choosing and delivering everyone's tree last year."

I smiled at the warm memory. "Yeah, we really did. So much has happened in the past year. In some ways if feels like last Christmas was years ago rather than just twelve short months, and in others it seems like it was just yesterday."

"Personally, I have a lot of very fond memories of Christmas last year." Cody took my hand in his. "I'm hoping, even with all the distractions, we can put our worries behind us and try to create some new memories this year."

I smiled at him. "I'll try." I looked around the café. There was a small tree in one corner which, combined with the holly strung everywhere, gave the place a festive feel. "I really do love this time of year. Everyone on the island seems to go all out with their decorations."

"I've been thinking about getting a small tree for the reception area of the newspaper. I don't have room for a display as grand as the one you and Tara created for the bookstore, but even a little holiday cheer will help brighten the place up."

"I think a tree would be nice."

"Hey, Cait; Cody," Holly, the waitress we were waiting for greeted us. "I heard you were asking about a man I waited on last Saturday."

I nodded. "The poor guy somehow ended up half dead on the beach. He has a pretty bad head injury and doesn't remember his name. I hoped he might have mentioned it to you."

Holly shook her head. "Sorry. He didn't say and I didn't ask. He did mention that he was on the island for a special holiday getaway. He was alone when he came in here and didn't say who his holiday guest was, but I assumed some lucky lady was meeting him here."

"So he didn't mention a woman's name?"

"No, he didn't. I will say that whoever that mystery woman is, she's one fortunate gal. Not only was the guy very nice and a total babe but he had a certain charm you don't seem to find in many men these days."

Despite the fact that the man had been barely conscious when I'd spoken with him, I'd had the same impression.

"Did he mention where he was staying?"

"He told me he'd rented a private cabin right on the water. He didn't mention where or who he rented it from, but there are only a few rental places on the island, so I guess you can check with each until you find the right one."

"Yeah, I will. And thanks for taking the time to chat with us."

"No problem. Are your choir kids going to do a Christmas play again this year? I went last year and it was adorable."

Cody and I were co-choir directors for the kids at St. Patrick's Catholic Church.

"We are, but we're doing it this next weekend instead of on Christmas weekend. We have a performance on Friday night and another one on Saturday night after the spaghetti dinner."

"I'll be there for sure. Y'all take care, now."

Cody and I paused while our food was served. Meanwhile, I'd grabbed the small notepad I kept in my backpack and started a list. I wrote down the victim as John Doe for now. Then I added the clues I wanted to follow up on, starting with Wilma Harold, the florist whose order form had been in the wallet I suspected was John Doe's. I hoped she'd have a name for me, but if not, I'd check the rental places in town that handled waterfront cabins. Whale Watch Rentals was just a few doors down from the florist, so I planned to go to the florist first, and then to Whale Watch Rentals, if need be.

I really hoped John Doe remembered who he was and how he came to be on the island alone, but if he didn't, I was going to do everything in my power to make sure he made it home for Christmas.

"So what time do you want to head to the tree lot?" I asked as we ate.

"I'll pick you up at the cabin at six. We'll grab some dinner first. I noticed the new seafood place on the pier is all decked out for the holiday. They even set up a Santa's village across from the restaurant that's large enough to walk through if it isn't raining."

"Sounds like fun. I could use a little Christmas magic right about now."

"Speaking of Christmas magic, I know we're committed to hosting a big holiday meal at Mr. Parsons's on Christmas Eve and Christmas Day with your family, but I'd like for the two of us to carve out some one-on-one time as well. Maybe a weekend away?"

I thought about it. Cody and I did seem to have a lot of obligations that involved other people, which seemed to leave very little time for just the two of us.

"I'd love that," I answered. "We have rehearsal for the play Wednesday and Thursday and the play itself on Friday and Saturday nights. Christmas is on Sunday, which sort of wipes out the following weekend as well. Maybe we could go somewhere for New Year's?"

"I could make that work. Did you have anywhere specific in mind?"

"I've been dreaming of a quaint cabin with a cozy fire, a snowy landscape, and maybe a sleigh ride through the forest. We won't have time to go too far, so maybe somewhere in the Cascades? I think Tara was planning on closing early on New Year's Eve anyway, New Year's is on a Sunday, we're closed Monday, and if history repeats, we'll be slow Tuesday and Wednesday, so maybe I can have Cassie cover for me and we can take five days. Can you get coverage at the newspaper?"

"Yeah, I can work it out. I'll look around to see if I can find anything. I think five days alone with you in an isolated cabin is exactly what I need to put the merry in my Christmas."

Chapter 3

Cody and I finished our meal, he returned to work, and I headed to the Coming Up Daisies Flower Shop. The cute building, with white trim and yellow shutters, was owned and operated by a woman I'd known for a good part of my life. Not only had Wilma Harold been a local for many years but she was in charge of arranging the flowers for the church where my family had worshipped since before I was born.

When I arrived at the shop Wilma was busy helping a customer, so I walked around, enjoying the colorful displays she'd created for the holiday season. Most of the arrangements were made up of a variety of evergreen branches accented with red and white flowers, although a few had pink and purple accents as well. Many of the arrangements had candles, while some featured ceramic figures such as jolly Santas or cheerful snowmen. I normally didn't bother buying flowers for my cabin because I had so many decorations already, but the scent provided by the fresh boutiques really couldn't be duplicated in any other way.

In addition to flowers, Wilma sold a variety of holiday-themed novelty items. I picked up a red and green elf hat and plopped it on my head. After the way my day had started I figured it couldn't hurt to add a little whimsy to my life.

"Afternoon, Wilma," I greeted her after the customer left.

"Caitlin, dear. How are you?"

"I'm good. Mostly. The reason I'm here is to ask you about a man who was in here on Saturday. He ordered two dozen roses."

"You must mean Prince Charming."

"Prince Charming?"

"Tall with dark hair and the bluest eyes you've ever seen?"

I thought of the haunted blue eyes of the man I'd found on the beach that morning. "Sounds right," I answered. "I'm afraid he's been injured."

"Oh, my. Is he okay?"

"Dr. Ryan says yes. The problem is that he suffered a head injury and hasn't been able to remember his name. I don't suppose he told you?"

Wilma frowned. "I don't remember him mentioning his name. He came in to order two dozen roses, a dozen red and a dozen white. Not an inexpensive purchase at this time of year. I asked if they were for someone special and he said they were, but he didn't elaborate. My assistant was here that day and she kiddingly wished her own prince charming would show up, and we've been referring to him as Prince Charming ever since."

"Did he pay with a credit card?"

"No, he paid with cash."

"How about a card to accompany the flowers? Did he write one?"

"No, he took the flowers with him and didn't ask for a card."

Rats. I'd really hoped Wilma knew something. "Did he say anything else? Where he was staying? Where he planned to dine that evening? Where he worked or what town he was from?"

"He said he'd rented a waterfront cabin, but he didn't say where. He did ask me to recommend a good place for dinner and I suggested Antonio's if he liked Italian."

I looked at my watch. Antonio's wouldn't be open yet, but I was certain Antonio would be there already, getting things ready for the evening.

"Oh, and he asked about a tree," Wilma added. "He wanted to get a tree for his cabin. I sent him over to the lot run by the St. Pat's Women's Guild."

"Thanks. I'll check both those places. For now, I'll just pay for the hat."

"It's on the house, dear. I do hope you figure out who Prince Charming is. He was such a nice man. I hate to think harm has come to him."

I called Finn as I left the shop to ask if he'd figured out John Doe's real name. He said he was heading over to the hospital to get a set of prints; so far no missing person's reports had come through that matched his description. I called the hospital to verify that he still hadn't remembered his name, then headed down the street to Whale Watch Rentals. As I walked, I looked up at the leaden sky. The rain had yet to return, but I had a feeling it was only a matter of time before the clouds overhead opened up to released their bounty.

"White Christmas" was playing in the background as I entered Whale Watch Rentals. The agency catered to high-end properties, so the interior of the shop was decorated in a tastefully sophisticated manner. Someone had set up a small white tree with pink ornaments in one corner, and the chairs in the waiting area were upholstered in white leather rather than the black vinyl found in shops around town.

"Can I help you?" a woman I didn't recognize asked.

"Is Franz here?"

"No. She's taking some time off to be with her family. If you're interested in a rental I'm sure I can find the perfect thing for your holiday getaway."

"Actually, I'm here looking for a man."

The woman looked scandalized. "I'm sorry, but we don't deal with that sort of rental."

"No, I don't want to rent a man. I need to identify one." I proceeded to explain to her the problem I was dealing with.

"And you say you don't know his name?"

"No. As I said, he can't remember."

She frowned. "I see. I'm not sure I can help you without a name or property address. And even if you had that, I don't think I should give out that sort of information. We do need to protect the privacy of our clients."

I supposed she had a point. Trying to track down a rental without a name was going to be next to impossible. Maybe I'd stop by the hospital to take a photo of the guy. Someone must know who John Doe is.

When I arrived at the hospital Dr. Ryan said it would be fine for me to visit with the man long enough to say hi and take a photo. He didn't want me wearing him out. I understood the doctor's concern, but I had about a hundred unanswered questions and hoped if I asked the right one something would spark a memory.

"You look better. Marginally." I smiled as I entered his room.

He grinned in return. He really did have a nice smile. "I was hoping you'd stop by. I was sure it must have been an angel at my side this morning, but I can see now it was an elf."

I reached up and touched the hat I still had on my head. "We elves do try to ensure that everyone has a happy holiday season."

"Well, whether you're an elf or an angel, I want to thank you for rescuing me."

I shrugged. "I'm glad we found you in time."

"We?"

"Me and Max and Clarence."

The man looked confused.

"The cat and dog who were with me."

"Of course. Please thank them for me too."

I walked farther into the room and sat down on the chair next to the bed. He was hooked up to an IV plus a variety of monitors, but his color had returned, so he no longer looked as if he were at death's door. "I'm only supposed to stay for a couple of minutes, so we'll need to talk fast. I don't suppose you've remembered your name?"

"No." He shook his head. "Everything is blank. I don't remember anything before you found me on the beach."

"I've been asking around and it seems you're on the island for a special holiday getaway. Ring a bell?"

He didn't answer, his face wearing the same look it had when I'd asked him his name.

"It seems you rented a cabin on the water. Do you remember where?"

"No. I'm sorry. Nothing you're saying sounds familiar."

"I don't suppose your name is Prince?"

"Prince?" He frowned.

"Never mind. I also found out you had lunch yesterday at the Driftwood Café and bought flowers at the Coming Up Daisies Flower Shop. Two dozen roses, one red, one white."

He just stared at me.

I turned as a nurse walked through the door and reminded me my time was up.

"I have to go, but I want you to know I'm working on figuring out who you are. I know it must be terrifying not to know."

"It is a bit unsettling."

"Try to get some rest. Maybe given a little time you'll start to remember. I'd best be on my way, but I'll keep asking around, and I'll come back to visit tomorrow. In the meantime, I'm going to show your photo around town to see if anyone remembers you." I stood up, snapped a photo, and followed the pushy nurse out of the room.

As I left the hospital, I called Finn again. He'd run John Doe's prints but so far hadn't found a match. I wanted to help track down his identity but wasn't sure where to take things next. I still had a couple of rental places to check, so I decided to start there and follow the clues wherever they led. First, however, I thought I'd drop in on Siobhan to see if she had news about the Coffee Cat Books loan.

I should have known when Siobhan greeted me with a hug that what she had to tell me wouldn't be good.

"You smell like peaches," Siobhan commented.

"New lotion." My stomach sunk as it became obvious she was stalling. Siobhan had never paid attention to my scented lotion in all the years we'd been sisters. "What did you find out about the loan?"

"I'm sorry, Cait. I tried everything I could think of to get the woman at Princeton Enterprises to put me in touch with her boss, but she wouldn't budge. I asked if I could leave a message in case he checked in and she said she was happy to take my number, but she highly doubted Mr. Princeton would return my call before returning to work after New Year's."

"Drat. I really hoped to have this worked out before Christmas. I'm afraid having this hanging over our heads is going to put a damper on the holiday. Do you think Finn might be able to track the guy down?"

"Track him down how?"

"I don't know. He's the deputy sheriff. He tracks people down for a living."

"Mr. Princeton hasn't broken any laws. Finn can't use law enforcement resources to track people down simply because his almost sister-in-law wants to speak to them."

I sighed. "Yeah, I guess you're right."

"I got a copy of your loan document from Tara. It looks like the bank did have the right to sell your loan and the owner of the loan has the right to call it in if you're late with your payment two out of any twelve-month period. I'm sorry, Cait, but unless Mr. Princeton can be persuaded to extend your loan there may not be much you can do."

I got up from the chair I'd been sitting in and began pacing around the room. "Did the woman at Princeton Enterprises tell you what Mr. Princeton plans to do with the property once he takes it away from us?"

Siobhan frowned. "Not specifically. I did ask, as the mayor, what sort of plans he had for the building, and while she wouldn't come right out and say it, she let it slip that he planned to give the building to his brother-in-law."

I kept pacing. I felt so helpless. I wanted to fix this for both Tara and myself, but I didn't know what more we could do.

"I've got some clues to follow up on the John Doe matter, but if you hear anything at all about the loan call me."

"I will." Siobhan hugged me again. "And don't worry. We'll figure something out."

There were three home and cabin rental outfits on the island: Whale Watch Rentals, High Tide Rentals, and Pelican

Bay Rentals. The temp at Whale Watch Rentals hadn't seemed to know who John Doe was, so I planned to check out High Tide Rentals next. The woman who ran that agency was a good friend of my mom's; I knew she'd tell me if she knew who John Doe was, confidentiality aside.

"The man you describe doesn't ring a bell. Have you tried the other agencies?" she asked.

"I haven't spoken to anyone at Pelican Bay Rentals yet. He must have rented the cabin through them."

"Not necessarily. There are a lot of property owners who handle their own rentals."

Terrific.

"Is there a way to track down individual landlords?"

"Anyone with a rental property on the island is supposed to register it with the island council for tax purposes. Some owners do; others operate under the table. If your John Doe didn't rent his cabin through one of the agencies it's going to be hard to track him down."

"Okay, well, thanks for your help. Maybe someone at Pelican Bay Rentals knows who he is."

No one did. I felt like I was at a standstill, but I did still have two clues to investigate: the Christmas tree lot and Antonio's. Cody and I were going to the tree lot after he got off work, so I went to Antonio's.

The restaurant was located in Harthaven. Madrona Island is made up of two distinct villages: Harthaven, to the north, where I grew up and most of the longtime families still lived, and Pelican Bay, to the south. Pelican Bay, where Coffee Cat Books was located, was a new development that had sprung up when the ferry began to provide service to the island. While Harthaven is a functional village with residential neighborhoods, a school, and practical stores such as a market, a drugstore, and a hardware store, Pelican Bay is a touristy type village, with art galleries, restaurants, B and Bs, and cute mom-and-pop shops, designed to meet the needs of our visitors.

Dining at Antonio's had been a tradition with my family since before I was born. I have many fond memories of meals after Mass on Sundays at the large table in the back when my dad was still alive and my siblings and I all still lived at home. I'm not sure why—maybe it was due to the handsome stranger who'd lost his memory or the loss of my childhood home the previous summer—but memories and family traditions were a big theme with me this holiday season.

I went around the back to the alley and entered Antonio's through the kitchen door because the restaurant wouldn't be open until dinner.

"Cait." Antonio greeted me with a hug. "What brings you here today?"

I took a deep breath and took in the scent of tomato sauce simmering on the stove before I answered. "I came to ask you about someone who might have been one of your customers. A tall man with dark hair who may have dined here over the weekend. I have a photo of him, but it was taken after he'd been injured, so I'm not sure you'll recognize him."

I showed Antonio my phone. "Sure, I remember him. He came in alone but ended up sharing his meal with a family of seven from Spokane."

"Did he seem to know the family before he came to eat?"

"No. Like I said, he came in alone. He asked for a table for one, but we were full. There was a group of seven at the eight top in the back, and one of them offered to let him join them. He accepted and they seemed to have had a wonderful time. The guy even picked up the tab for the entire table and left a good tip too."

"That was nice of him."

"I had a feeling he enjoyed the company."

"Did he pay by credit card?"

"Cash."

How much money was the guy carrying around anyway?

"Did he mention his name?"

Antonio paused. "No. At least not to me. He did say he had family in Italy. An uncle, I think. Seems like the relative's last name was Pizzano."

I supposed it was possible John Doe's last name was Pizzano. He did look like he could have Italian blood. Of course if the relative who lived in Italy was an uncle, he could have a completely different last name.

"Do you know if the people the man sat with are still on the island?"

"No. They said they were leaving the next day, which would have been yesterday."

"That's too bad. I bet our John Doe mentioned his name to them while they were eating."

"I do remember him saying something about a Christmas tree and needing to buy ornaments. I'm pretty sure the mother of the family suggested the Christmas store in town."

"I guess I can try there. Thanks for taking the time to talk to me. I know you're busy."

"I'm never too busy for you, *cara mia*. I wish I could be of more help. He seemed like a nice guy. I hope he can find the memories he's lost."

"Yeah." I signed. "Me too."

Chapter 4

Walking into a store filled from floor to ceiling with everything Christmas was like entering Santa's Village in the North Pole. Every tree was covered in lights and ornaments and every available table, counter, and shelf was loaded down with decorations that moved, flashed, danced, and sang carols.

I hadn't thought a store dedicated only to Christmas would do very well on our small island, but the proprietor had set up displays and minivillages throughout that would keep children and adults alike fascinated for hours on end.

"Oh, look; we have the same hat," a young woman dressed as an elf from head to toe said to me.

"We do, but it looks like you have the whole outfit."

"Comes with the job. Can I help you?"

I held my phone up for her to see the photo. "Have you seen this man?"

A look for horror crossed her face. "My God. What happened to him?"

I turned the phone around and considered the photo I'd snapped. I guess I could understand her response. John Doe had a white bandage wrapped around his head and facial bruising I hadn't noticed that morning had darkened considerably.

"He was injured. I have reason to believe he might have been in this store at some time over the weekend. He's tall, maybe six foot two. He has dark brown hair and the bluest eyes I've ever seen."

"Oh, him," she gushed. "Who could help but remember a guy like that? Not only was he movie-star handsome but he was just about the nicest man I've ever met. I'm sure he must be married, but if it turns out he's single, he's exactly the type of guy I'd latch on to and never let go."

"Did he happen to mention his name?"

She frowned. "You have a photo of him, but you don't know his name?"

I explained how I'd met him and why I wanted to know his name.

"Wow, amnesia. I never knew anyone with who really had amnesia before."

"So his name..." I brought us back on topic. "Did he mention it?"

"Not that I remember. He came in and bought a bunch of lights and ornaments. You could tell he didn't have anything, which I commented on, and he explained that he was on the island for a holiday and hadn't brought decorations with him. He spent over four hundred bucks."

"Did he pay with a credit card?"

"Cash. And he left a tip for all us elves who were working that day so we could order in dinner. We were supposed to close at six, but we've been staying until well after eight with all the holiday traffic."

"Do you remember if he mentioned where he was staying?"

The girl furrowed her brow as she appeared to be considering the question. "He said something about a cabin, but he didn't say where it was."

"Do you remember anything else that might help me track down his identity? Where he was visiting from or who might be staying with him?"

"He asked about a toy store, so I'm guessing he's here with at least one kid. And he also asked about a jewelry store, so maybe he was traveling with a wife and kid."

"Did you recommend stores to him?"

"I gave him directions to Sullivan's Toys in Harthaven and the addresses for three stores that sell jewelry: Pelican Bay Jewelers, O'Connell's Jewelry Store, and Rocks and Riches."

I knew where Sullivan's Toys was, as well as all three jewelers; it wouldn't be too hard to follow up with them if need be.

"Okay, thank you. I work down the street at Coffee Cat Books. If you think of anything else will you call me?"

"Sure. I'd like to help if I can."

I didn't have a lot of time before I had to meet up with Cody, so I headed in that direction. Visits to the toy and jewelry stores would have to wait for another day.

Cody and I wandered around the tree lot hand in hand. We'd gotten a late start so we'd just grabbed burgers rather than stopping at the new seafood place as we'd planned. I'd worn my elf hat and brought a Santa hat for Cody so, on the surface, we looked like a normal couple out for a romantic evening, not clueless sleuths hoping to come up with the one piece of information that would blow our investigation wide open. I'd checked in with Finn again; he hadn't had any luck matching John Doe's prints to a person. Almost everyone who arrived on the island came by ferry, so he was having copies of the ferry surveillance tapes sent to him for the past few days. Maybe if he found out exactly when he'd gotten here we could narrow our search. Finn suggested that Cody run an article in the midweek newspaper, asking if anyone knew the identity of our John Doe or had any information that could help us track down his name. In the meantime, we agreed there wasn't any reason to assemble the Scooby gang; so far, there really wasn't a crime to solve.

"I'm sorry you had a frustrating day," Cody comforted me.

"It has been frustrating. I want to help John Doe, but we have so little to go on. Wilma from the flower shop said he was asking about a Christmas tree and sent him here. Maybe he had one delivered."

"It wouldn't hurt to ask."

The weather had cleared for the moment and the tree lot was festively lit and decorated. Although we had six trees to find, purchase, and deliver, I decided to let Cody get started while I asked around to find out if anyone remembered speaking to John Doe. The first two women I spoke to hadn't been working on Saturday, but the third volunteer, Marley Donnelly, my Aunt Maggie's best friend and business partner, had been working and remembered him. First I explained what I needed to know and why.

"What a darn shame," Marley said over the sound of carols playing in the background. "Such a nice young man. So polite and patient. He was here to find the perfect tree for someone special, and I think he looked at every tree in the lot before he finally settled on one."

"Did he happen to give you his name?"

Marley thought about it. "I don't remember him mentioning it. We chatted for a while, and I remember him being very sweet and charming. Not only did he leave us a nice tip but he left a sizable donation for the church as well. I do hope the poor man is going to be all right."

"Dr. Ryan says he'll be fine, but it's important that we find out who he is. Can you think of anything at all that might help us?"

"He asked about buying decorations for the tree and I referred him to the Christmas store in Pelican Bay."

I already knew he'd gone to the Christmas store, and now I knew he'd gone there after buying his tree here. "Did he mention where he was staying?" I stepped aside as a family of five rushed by as they homed in on the perfect tree.

"No. After he paid for the tree he tied it on the top of his car and left. He was driving a blue sedan, if that helps. I think it was a Mercedes. Yes, I'm sure of it."

"Did you catch a license plate?"

"No. It never occurred to me to look. Although..." Marley paused. It looked like she was trying to retrieve a reluctant memory. "Now that I think about it, I don't think the car had regular plates. I think it had one of those paper dealer plates you find on new cars. Yes," Marley nodded, "I'm sure of it."

"Do you remember which dealership?" We didn't have any on the island, so John Doe most likely would have purchased the car before he arrived here.

"No. I'm sorry. I really didn't pay all that much attention."

"Thanks for your help. I already spoke to an elf at the Christmas store and I'll follow up with some stores she told him about tomorrow. I really want to help him, but right now I have six trees to pick out."

"I set one aside for Maggie," Marley said. "She told me you and Cody were going to be here tonight, and when the new shipment arrived I snagged one I knew would be just right for her."

I hugged Marley. "I appreciate that. Now I just have Mom, Francine, Mr. Parsons, Cody, and myself to find trees for."

"It looks like Cody has found a few. I'll grab a sales sheet so he can start loading them. You can settle up once we have them all ready to go."

Thanks to Marley's help, our task took half the time it might have, which meant

Cody and I might have some alone time if the deliveries didn't take too long. We stacked the trees in the back of his truck in the order of delivery: first my mom's, because Mr. Parsons, Cody, Aunt Maggie, Francine, and I all lived on the peninsula.

"The trick is going to be to spend just the right amount of time at my mom's," I coached him. "If we aren't careful she'll lead us into a long conversation that will cut into our couple time, but if we try to leave too soon we'll ignite her you-never-come-to-visit speech."

"We have dinner with your mom almost every Sunday."

"I know. But dinner somehow doesn't count. She keeps track of the amount of time we each spend with her lately, and if she feels it isn't sufficient she'll go out of her way to let us know."

"Do you think she's lonely since her engagement ended?"

Did I? I wasn't sure. On one hand, Dad had been gone for quite a while, so you'd think she'd be used to being without a man, but she had seemed to blossom during her disaster of an engagement; maybe her dip into the romance pool had reminded her of what she was missing. After the house had burned down she and Cassie had moved in with Maggie, but now that it was just the two of them in a tiny condo, maybe she *was* lonely and I just hadn't stopped to realize it.

"I guess it wouldn't hurt to stay for hot cocoa," I amended. "You might have a point about the lonely thing. After the fire Aiden got his own place, and I know Cassie is hardly ever home."

Cody took my hand and gave it a squeeze. Most boyfriends wouldn't care about the loneliness of their girlfriend's mother, but Cody wasn't most boyfriends; he was the *best* boyfriend.

When we walked into the condo Mom and Cassie lived in I knew Cody might be right. Normally Mom started decorating the day after Thanksgiving, but here it was, less than two weeks until Christmas, and there wasn't a decoration in sight.

"Thank you for the tree, dear," Mom greeted me as we walked in through the front door. "While I do appreciate the sentiment, I'm not sure where to put it."

"I know you said you didn't want a tree, but Cassie really wants one." I looked around the room. It was going to be a tight fit, but we'd manage. "How about we move that chair in the corner? We'll put it in the bedroom for now. I think the tree will look really nice by that window."

"I don't have lights. Or even a stand."

"I've got you covered." Cody handed my mom a large box from the Christmas store. "It's just some lights and a few things to get you started. I figured you'd want to pick out the bulk of the decorations for yourself."

Okay, now I felt like the worst daughter in the world. I hadn't even stopped to think about decorations, but apparently my wonderfully thoughtful boyfriend had and had taken the time to buy my mother what she'd need to make her tree bright and colorful.

Mom wiped a tear from her eye after she opened the box Cody had picked up for her. "Thank you so much. This is wonderful, although it won't be the same without Great-Great-Grandma Hart's tree topper."

Mom had a point. Great-Great-Grandma Hart's tree topper had been a family tradition for generations.

"It won't be the same, but that doesn't mean you can't still have a beautiful tree," I said encouragingly. "How about if I pick you up tomorrow on my lunch hour and take you to the Christmas store to pick up a topper? I'll even throw in lunch at the Driftwood."

Mom smiled a sort of half smile that didn't quite reach her eyes, but she agreed to my plan.

"Would you like to stay for cocoa?" Mom asked.

I was about to say no but changed my mind. "We'd love to. Maybe we should discuss our plans for Christmas Eve and Christmas Day while we're at it."

Mom's smile grew bigger. "I'd like that."

"We're planning a Christmas Eve party at Mr. Parsons's again and of course the entire Hart clan is invited," I began.

Mom's mood lightened significantly as we discussed the menu for Christmas Eve and the pros and cons of asking Aunt Maggie to host Christmas dinner. Mom had always hosted the dinner, but there was no way the entire Hart family could fit into her tiny condo. While it was true that Mom no longer needed a six-bedroom house, we all agreed that at some point we were going to have to find Mom a place with a larger kitchen. Cody suggested that maybe a small house with only a couple of bedrooms but a large living area would be a good option. Mom seemed to warm to the idea, and he and I promised to help her look around after the first of the year.

After we left Mom's we headed to Francine's, where we were given another cup of cocoa and another plate of cookies. Tree delivery, as it turned out, had become a fattening activity. If I was going to have lunch with my mother the following day I'd better skip breakfast altogether.

As he had with my mom's tree, Cody set Francine's in her stand. He wasn't only the perfect boyfriend; he was the perfect friend and neighbor.

"It's perfect, simply perfect," Francine gushed. I stood beside her to admire the beautiful fir while cuddling Francine's cat Romeo, who had come to the peninsula as my very first magical cat.

"I'm glad you love it. Cody worked really hard to find the perfect tree for everyone."

"He did a wonderful job." Francine clasped her hands in front of her chest. "You know, I think this is shaping up to be the best Christmas I've had in a very long time."

It made me feel happy that Francine was so happy.

"I've been working on the menu for the Christmas Eve dinner at Mr. Parsons's all day. I can't wait to try out a couple of new side dishes I'm working on."

"Can you be sure to include my mom in the planning?" I asked. "I think she's feeling a little displaced this year."

"Absolutely. I'll call her this evening. I have a feeling this party is going to be the event of the season. I spoke to Mr. Parsons and he seems to be as excited as I am. He even asked if I would help him select and wrap gifts to give out to everyone who joins us."

"That's nice of him."

"He doesn't have any family and up until last year, I think he mostly endured solitary Christmases. By organizing the Christmas Eve event, you and Cody have given him a reason to plan and prepare for the arrival of the holiday. I can't tell you how hard it is to reignite the feeling of anticipation you felt as a child once you get on in years."

Mr. Parsons's party last year had started off as an attempt by Cody and me to bring some Christmas magic into the old man's life. Initially it was just going to be the three of us, but by the time Christmas Eve had rolled around we'd served over thirty meals and a new tradition had been born.

"I'm glad we can bring some joy to Mr. Parsons's life, and I, too, am looking forward to the event." I hugged Francine.

"It's so nice of you to help him with his plans for host gifts."

"It's no problem at all. Helping him has served to bring some anticipation into my own mostly solitary life."

After we left Francine's we headed to Aunt Maggie's. As Marley had guessed, Maggie adored the tree we dropped off for her. Cody helped settle it in the stand and carry the ornaments down from the attic. She explained that both Father Kilian and Sister Mary had agreed to come over and help her decorate the following day. Father Kilian planned to announce his plans to retire to the congregation after the first of the year. And while he and Maggie weren't going to announce their plans to marry for a couple of years after that, he wanted to fill Sister Mary in on the situation because they'd worked side by side for so many years. Maggie insisted she should be present for Father Kilian's talk with Sister Mary; thus the plan for the pair to join Maggie for dinner and tree trimming was born.

After dropping my own tree at the cabin, we headed next door to help Mr. Parsons get his set up. Cody carried down the decorations and strung the lights for Mr. Parsons's tree and we realized it was pretty late. I was reluctant to do so, but I found myself suggesting couple time might need to wait.

"How about I come over tomorrow after work and help you put up your tree?" Cody suggested. "I'll bring some wine and takeout from Antonio's."

"Sounds perfect. Do you think you can stay?"

Cody kissed me gently on the lips. "I think that can be arranged, although I do need to get up early to get the midweek edition of the paper buttoned up."

"Did you run the article about John Doe?"

"Finn and I talked about it some more and decided to wait to post a photo until he can follow up on a few clues. While posting a photo may lead to the man's identity, it could bring out a lot of kooks as well. The guy seemed to have been throwing around a lot of cash and it occurred to Finn that opening the door to anyone who might want to claim the guy as a long-lost brother or uncle might not be the best idea. Besides, it's been less than a day since you found him. Finn is still hoping that after a good night's sleep he'll wake up and remember on his own."

"I suppose there's a good possibility that could happen."

"Come on; I'll take you home," Cody offered.

"I don't suppose you can stay tonight..." I said persuasively.

"I'd love nothing more, but I already told Mr. Parsons I'd help him finish the tree when I got back."

"But tomorrow?"

"I'm all yours."

I liked the sound of that.

Chapter 5

Tuesday, December 13

I woke early the next morning and took Max for a quick run before I got ready for work. With the holiday approaching, it had been busier than usual at the bookstore, and I knew Tara wouldn't appreciate it if I was late. Having strong sales over the holidays really made a difference as to how comfortable our cash flow would be during the slow winter months, providing we still had a bookstore to worry about.

The rain we'd been having off and on seemed to have taken a hiatus, but the feel of the air was definitely cooler than it had been. If the moisture returned while the temperatures were still hovering in the low thirties we might actually get some magical Christmas snow.

I tried to focus on the week ahead while I ran. It was going to be a busy one, with holiday chores and community plans. Cody and I would be busy with play rehearsals the following two nights, followed by the opening of the St. Patrick's Church Christmas play on Friday and a repeat following the annual spaghetti dinner on Saturday. Sunday was usually spent with family and friends, which left very little time to deal with the shopping, baking, and decorating that still needed to be done.

And somewhere, between work and holiday plans, I wanted to help John Doe find the memories he seemed to have lost with a single blow to the head. Memories are often the only things we have left as our lives near their natural conclusion. I remembered when my own grandmother had approached her final years she often couldn't remember what she'd had for breakfast, but she could remember what she was wearing the day Kennedy was shot or the feel of the sun on her back the first time she met my grandfather. How sad it would be to lose the part of ourselves that makes us *us*.

"So what do you think, Max? Should we head back?"

Max didn't answer, but he did turn around, so I guessed he agreed. I was already anticipating a busy day at the beginning of an even busier week, which left me feeling sort of angsty when what I wanted to feel on this cold winter morning was happy and content.

"You're early," Tara said as I entered the bookstore with a Santa hat on my head.

"I know that fact both thrills and amazes you, but I remembered we still needed to do the restocking."

"Look at you, developing a work ethic."

I felt proud that Tara noticed.

"Any news after I spoke to you yesterday?" I asked.

"In regard to our loan, no. However, in regard to my sanity, yes."

"Yes good or yes bad?"

"Bad. An hour after talking to you, my mom showed up at my doorstep."

Yikes. Tara and her mother didn't get along.

"How did it go?"

"It was tense. Very tense. I don't know why we can't seem to get along," Tara complained. "She's a good person who seems to get along with everyone else, but when it comes to me it seems everything out of her mouth is a thinly veiled insult. I wanted to tell her about the loan fiasco. It would have been nice to have someone offer comfort at a time when it seems my life is crumbling around me. But I knew if I told her what had happened she'd spend the rest of the day berating me for paying the loan late twice in a twelve-month period in the first place."

"She does tend to enjoy a good lecture."

"Yeah, but only when she's lecturing me. She's pretty tolerant of the mistakes others make."

I used a box cutter to open a box of greeting cards. "I think difficult relationships are just part of the parent/child paradigm. I don't always get along with my mom, and I know the main reason Siobhan moved to Seattle in the first place was because she couldn't deal with Mom. Danny argued with my dad constantly, and although Aiden and Dad had more in common, they also had their share of problems. If you ask me, tension in the parent/child relationship seems to be the natural order of things."

"Maybe, but I feel like mine are worse than most."

"I kind of doubt that's true."

"Really? When my mom showed up at my front door she hugged me and then announced that she was going to take me shopping and to get my hair cut because I obviously hadn't gotten around to fixing myself up since the last time she visited."

"Ouch." I knew Tara had been to the hairdresser just last week.

"Then she was barely in the door when she commented that she hadn't liked the carpet I'd picked out for my living area when she'd first seen it, but it seemed to mask the cat hair better than some colors, so maybe it was a good choice after all. I had my carpets professionally cleaned in anticipation of the cookie exchange next week two days ago. There wasn't a cat hair in sight and yet she had to comment."

"I know it's hard for you when your mom visits, but she's gone now," I offered. "She is gone now?"

Tara sighed. "Yeah. It was a quick visit. She left on the first ferry this morning. I just don't know why we can't get along better. I really try, but the more I try to find a common ground with her the more it feels like I'm trying to mix oil and water. Shouldn't mothers and daughters have something in common?"

I glanced away, unable to maintain eye contact with Tara. It was hard knowing the truth behind her parentage. It somehow felt wrong that I knew this very important thing about her that I'd sworn never to tell her or anyone else.

"So, any news about your mystery man?" Tara asked.

"No. I feel so bad for him. I'm hoping his memory comes back on its own and he can get on with his life. Dr. Ryan seems to think that physically he'll be ready to leave the hospital as early as tomorrow."

"It must be so terrifying to wake up in a strange place and have no memory of who you are or what's happened to you. Do you have a plan in the event he doesn't remember on his own?"

"I have a few things to follow up on today that I hope will lead to answers. In fact, I was hoping to take a long lunch. I not only need to follow up on some leads, but I need to take my mom to buy a tree topper." I explained about our Christmas tree delivery to the condo the previous evening.

"Sure. No problem. I feel so bad for your mom. It's hard to lose everything that's meant so much to you."

"Yeah. Losing the house was hard for all of us, but especially for Mom. She moved into that house as a young bride, and it was in that house that she raised five children and lived with my father until he died. I know she had a cavalier attitude about selling when the fiancé from hell convinced her that she should, but deep down I think she loved that house and everything in it. Now, since the fire destroyed everything, it's almost as if her memories are gone as well. It's really sad."

"She may have lost the house and the items that represented the mementos of her life, but she still has her memories. No one can take those."

"Tell that to John Doe."

"Good point. By the way, did you ask Cassie about working at the bookstore part time when school is out for the holiday? I think we're going to have a busy couple of weeks."

"I did and she's in. She says can start on Friday. She has one test to take in the morning and then she's done until school resumes in January, which is fortunate because Cody and I are talking about getting away for New Year's and I was hoping to take a couple of extra days off."

"No problem. It usually dies here after New Year's. I'm sure Cassie and I can handle things. Where are you going?"

"Cody is taking care of the reservations, but I suggested somewhere snowy, isolated, and romantic."

"It sounds like heaven."

"Yeah, it really does. Did we order more of these Christmas mugs? I think this is the last box."

"They should arrive with today's shipment. I ordered more of the handcrafted Christmas stockings as well. It seems like the novelty items are almost selling better than the books."

"A lot of people have made the transition to eBooks," I pointed out.

"I guess that's true. And I kind of get why eBooks are so popular. They can be less expensive and they don't take up any room. Plus, they're easier to carry around with you. But I do worry about the overall affect if hardcover books eventually go the way of the fax machine and fade away completely."

"What do you mean?"

Tara shrugged. "I don't know exactly. I guess I just think about the long-term result of such a huge change. Without books in physical form, used books will eventually cease to exist, and there will come a time when we'll no longer have the thrill of finding an undiscovered treasure in a secondhand bookstore."

I hadn't thought of that. There was nothing better than digging through old volumes faded with age in the hope of finding something truly special. "I personally enjoy the convenience of an eBook, but physical books and bookstores such as ours will always hold a special place in my heart."

A look of desolation came over Tara's face.

"You're thinking about the loan," I said.

"What if we can't work it out? We have so many plans for this place. So many wonderful plans. It will be so incredibly sad if we don't get the chance to try them out."

"We'll manage things somehow," I assured Tara.

"How?"

"I don't know. Siobhan is looking in to a few things. She's smart and she's an excellent negotiator. I know she'll figure something out if she can ever get hold of Anthony Princeton."

"Did she find out why he wants this building in the first place?"

"It seems he's planning on giving it to his brother-in-law. Siobhan didn't know what he's planning to do with it."

"This whole thing is just too depressing." Tara began to set up the coffee bar in anticipation of the first ferry of the day.

"It looks like the ferry is docking. I'll grab some more cups while you start another pot of coffee."

As we expected, the ferry brought in a brisk business, and before I knew it, it was time to meet my mother for lunch and tree-topper shopping. I decided that no matter how much she drove me crazy today I was going to make a commitment to be sensitive to her feelings and try to be patient and understanding.

"Maybe you should make something," I suggested to her as she looked at and discarded *every* tree topper in the Christmas store. "Great-Great-Grandma Hart's topper wasn't only old; it was handmade. I think in part that's what made it so special. I know all of your sewing and crafting supplies were destroyed in the fire, but I bet Maggie would be happy to help you make something really special."

Aunt Maggie owned the Bait and Stitch, a unique shop that sold fishing supplies as well as sewing and quilting ones. She was a creative woman who could make something wonderful out of nothing at all.

"Perhaps a handmade topper would be better," Mom mused. "Nothing we've seen so far seems quite right for our tree."

"I need to stop by Sullivan's Toy Store for a few minutes. How about I drop you at the Bait and Stitch so you can talk to Maggie about a tree topper, and then I'll pick you up and drop you at home when I'm finished."

"The toy store? There haven't been any children in the family for quite some time."

I didn't want to mention the situation with John Doe to my mother. I could already imagine the lecture I'd receive about befriending strangers, so I simply told her I wanted to buy a gift for a friend's baby and left it at that.

"That's nice, but Sullivan's is in Harthaven. Are you sure you want to drive all the way over there and then have to come back to get me?"

"It won't take all that long. Besides, this will give you a chance to visit with Maggie. I bet she'll even make you tea."

"Whatever you want to do is fine with me."

Sullivan's was small in comparison to the big-lot stores that could be found in Seattle, but the toys they carried were of good quality and tended to speak to the imagination in a way electronic devices never did. I didn't have any children to buy toys for most of the time, but I enjoyed browsing the aisles of unique offerings that included both traditional things like dolls and toy trucks, as well as others designed to create a learning experience for kids.

"Hey, Cait," Joy Holiday, the store owner, greeted me. "What can I help you find today?"

I watched as the jingle bells on Joy's hat bounced when she spoke. There was nowhere better than a toy store at Christmas. "I actually just had a couple of questions I hoped you could answer for me."

"I'd be happy to if I can."

I thought about showing Joy the photo I'd taken of John Doe, then remembered the look on the face of the elf at the Christmas store, so instead I just asked about the tall, dark-haired man with the beautiful blue eyes.

"Yeah, I remember him. He was in on Saturday. He was looking for something special for a seven-year-old girl."

"Did he happen to mention his name?"

Joy scrunched her mouth to one side as she thought about it. "No, I don't think so. The girl he was shopping for is named Hannah, but I don't remember him giving me his own name."

"Did he pay with a credit card?"

"Cash."

"Did he mention where he was staying, or if he might have been on the island with someone else, maybe Hannah's mother?"

Joy leaned her elbows on the counter and looked me in the eye. "Why are you so interested in this guy? Is everything okay between you and Cody?"

"Everything's fine. It's just that the man I'm asking about has had an accident." Now I held up my phone.

A look of horror crossed Joy's face. "Wow. That looks bad."

"He's wasn't hurt all that bad despite the way he looks, but he does seem to have amnesia. I'm trying to help him figure out who he is."

"Amnesia. Wow, that sounds serious. I'd totally freak out if I got hurt and didn't know who I was. Talk about a shock. I'd love to help you figure this out, but I really don't think he ever mentioned his name."

"Did you get the feeling Hannah was here on the island with him?"

"No. At least not at the time he was here. I'm not sure what the situation was—I imagine a messy divorce—but I got the impression he hadn't seen her in quite some time and wanted to get her something really special for Christmas."

"Okay, thanks. If you think of anything else call me."

I called Finn to let him know John Doe might have a seven-year-old daughter named Hannah and, if he did, he was most likely estranged from the girl's mother. I wasn't sure how this would help us identify him, but I figured every piece of information, no matter how small, could help us discover his identity.

The clues I was tracking down weren't getting me anywhere, so I decided to go to the hospital to speak to John Doe again. I didn't want to upset him or cause him to panic, but I needed to see if he'd been able to remember anything that could help us figure out what was going on.

He grinned when I walked into his room. "I was wondering if you'd make it back."

"I said I would and I always keep my promises. You seem to be feeling better today."

"A lot better. In fact, the doctor said I was well enough to leave the hospital tomorrow if there was someone to release me to. He isn't comfortable with just letting me fend for myself, which I'm thankful for."

"Is your memory coming back at all?" I asked. "Even tiny glimpses?"

He frowned. "Sometimes I feel as if there might be something. Nothing concrete; more like the shadow of a memory. I get this flash of something, but then it's gone. It's there, but I just can't reach it."

"Does the name Hannah mean anything to you?"

A look of pain flashed across his face and then it was gone. "Should it?"

"I don't know. I spoke to the woman who owns a toy store in town and she said you were in there on Saturday, buying gifts for a seven-year-old named Hannah."

He paused. "Do you think I'm married? Might Hannah be my child?"

"I don't know. You didn't elaborate about your situation to the toy shop owner." I looked at his hand. "You aren't wearing a ring. I suppose you could be divorced."

He made a face that revealed how little he thought of the idea.

"Do you remember anything at all about your time on Madrona Island prior to my finding you on the beach? A building, a setting? A sound, a smell? Anything?"

"Rain. I remember the sound of rain."

It had been raining the morning I'd found him on the beach, so that didn't necessarily mean anything.

"And a sweet smell. Not like sugar; more like flowers."

It totally amazed me that he could remember what flowers smelled like and rain sounded like but couldn't remember his own name.

I held up the key I'd found in the wallet I was pretty sure belonged to him. "Does this look familiar?"

"It's a key."

"Yes, but the key to what?"

He stared at it, but I didn't notice any sign of recognition on his face.

"Prior to whatever happened to you, you bought two dozen flowers, one red roses, one white. Can you remember why you bought them or who you bought them for?"

He furrowed his brow. "I really have no idea."

"I suppose you could have had a date, but you didn't mention one or a wife to the florist."

"I'm sorry. I really wish I could help, but I can't. As I said, whatever memories I have are still out of reach. I think the flowers might have meaning, but I don't know why. When I picture roses I think of death."

If roses represented death to him, it seemed odd that he'd buy them in the first place. If there was some special significance, it must be something else.

"You said you remembered hearing the rain," I continued. "Do you remember any other sounds?"

"It wasn't rain. It sounded like rain, but it wasn't raining. It was something else."

"Maybe a dripping faucet?"

He shook his head. "No. Not a faucet."

"A sprinkler, or maybe water dripping from a surface?"

"No, I don't think so." He closed his eyes, then shook his head. "I'm sorry. The memory is just beyond my grasp."

"Yeah, I get that when I'm trying to remember someone's name. It makes me nuts. This situation must really be making you crazy."

"You have no idea. I really want to help you, but I can't seem to get to where I need to be."

"It's okay. We'll figure it out." I wrote down my cell number on a piece of paper. "If you think of anything, anything at all, call me. Either way, I'll be back tomorrow and we can talk some more then."

"Do you know what's going to happen to me? If I don't get my memory back? I tried to ask the doctor, but he just got a strange look on his face and assured me that I'd be taken care of."

"Honestly? I'm not sure what's going to happen if your memory doesn't come back. Finn and Dr. Ryan are good men and they want to help you. I'm sure there's a solution and I'm equally certain we'll find it."

Chapter 6

I went back to the bookstore after I left the hospital. There wasn't anything I could do right then that wasn't already being done by someone else and I knew Tara needed the help. When I entered the store through the alley I saw things were worse than I'd expected.

"Where did all these people come from?" The bookstore was completely packed, the line at the coffee counter wrapped around the main display and out the door.

"The ferry. Grab a pad and start taking orders. I'm working as fast as I can."

I wrapped an apron around my waist and headed to the cash register. "What can I get you?" I asked the first person in line.

"A double pump white mocha with soy milk, no foam, extra whip, and a triple shot espresso with a splash of nonfat milk and a sprinkle of cinnamon."

"Coming right up. That will be eight dollars. You can pick it up at the end of the counter. Next?"

By the time Tara and I had served the last of the tourists who had descended on us like locusts during the Rapture, we were both exhausted.

"Is there a special event in town?" I asked. Normally a Tuesday, even in December, was a slowish day.

"I don't know. When all those people got off the ferry and headed this way I couldn't believe what I was seeing. There must have been a special tour we didn't know about."

I looked around at the mess the crowd had left behind. It looked like Tara and I were going to be staying later than expected.

"Let's put out the Closed sign and tackle this mess," I suggested. "It's almost closing anyway, and Cody and I have a date planned, so I don't want to be too late."

"Sounds like a good plan. How'd it go at the hospital?"

I began picking up trash and wiping down tabletops as I explained John Doe's general physical and mental health.

"It seems like he's doing better."

"Physically the doctor seems to think he's ready to be checked out. His memory, though, is as foggy as ever. He did comment about remembering the sound of rain."

"It's been raining off and on for days," Tara said.

"Yeah, but he said he remembered the sound but it wasn't raining at the time. I asked if it might have been a leaky faucet or sprinklers he was remembering, but he didn't think that was it."

"It's no wonder the poor man's memories are scrambled after everything he's been through. It's entirely possible the rain he thinks he remembers is a memory that's months or even years old."

"That could be true. I keep thinking how frustrated I get when I can't remember someone's name or some random fact I know the answer to but can't quite grasp. He must feel that way every minute of the day."

Tara began breaking down the coffee machine so it could be cleaned. "I really do feel for him. I hate it when I see an actor on TV and can't quite remember where I'd seen him before, or when I run into an old friend and her name is on the tip of my tongue but I can't quite think of it. Do you have any idea what he's going to do if his memory *doesn't* come back?"

"I'm not sure. I'm really trying to figure out what his name is. If I can do that, maybe he'll come up with the rest."

"I hope so."

"Are you doing book club tomorrow night?"

"Yes," Tara answered. "But then we're taking three weeks off for the holidays. We're having a party after if you want to join us."

"Choir," I reminded her.

"Oh, that's right. How's the play coming along?"

I began straightening bookshelves as I answered. "I think it's going to be awesome. The kids are really excited and it seems like all of them have been practicing their lines. I have some photos of the costumes in my backpack if you want to see them."

"I'd love to."

I went into the office to retrieve the backpack I used like a purse. I took it out to the front and set it on the counter. I removed a few items from the top of the backpack to get to the prints of the photos I'd copied.

"Check out the costumes for the baby sheep." I held up the first photo.

"That's really cute, but aren't all your choir members too big for that?"

"We recruited a few of their younger siblings. Oh, and look at the halos we made for the angels."

I continued to show Tara the photos, which led to conversations about each and every member of the cast. Before I knew it, I was late for my evening with Cody.

"Oh, geez, I need to run."

"Go ahead. I'll lock up."

"Thanks. I owe you one." I grabbed my stuff off the counter, found my keys, and headed into the cat lounge to grab the cats I'd brought to feature that day. I'd drop them at the cat sanctuary and then hope I still had time to change before Cody arrived.

"I'm sorry I'm late." Cody kissed me when he arrived at my cabin. "I had an anonymous tip that Bruce Drysdale was seen at Shots over the weekend, so I went to check it out."

Shots was a bar on the very west end of Pelican Bay. While it was ten miles away from my cabin by car, it wasn't all that far from the peninsula where we lived via the beach. The establishment was a drinker's bar that specialized in generous shots of top-quality hard liquor.

"Who's Bruce Drysdale?" I asked.

"He's the man I told you about who the state police believe is responsible for the string of bank robberies across Idaho and Washington."

"You went to interview him?"

"No. But I did head over to Shots to interview the bartender and show him a photo the press has been circulating the past week. He could confirm that the man in the photo was at the bar on both Saturday and Sunday nights. Once I verified the tip, I headed over to Finn's office to fill him in. Then we got to chatting about the case, which is why I'm late."

"Do you think the man is still on the island?" I wondered.

"I don't know. Finn has notified the Washington State Ferry system to keep an eye out for him and has issued an all-points bulletin for the county as well. Chances are the guy has moved on. It wouldn't be smart for him to stay in one place too long when so many people are looking for him. Anyway, let's eat before our food gets cold."

Cody set out the to-go boxes while I opened a bottle of wine. We sat at the kitchen table and watched the rain, which had returned. The forecast was for rain off and on over the next several days.

"How did your own sleuthing go today?" Cody asked when we'd settled in.

"It was pretty much a bust. I followed up on the clues I had, but I don't seem to be getting anywhere. Everyone I spoke to agreed John Doe was extremely charming and charismatic and that he not only left a large tip pretty much everywhere he went but paid cash as well. Not a single person remembers him giving his name, although Joy from the toy store did say he mentioned a seven-year-old named Hannah."

"God, I hope there isn't a little girl waiting for her dad to come home."

"I thought of that, but Joy seemed to think Hannah wasn't on the island at that time. It seemed to her that she planned at some point to visit him. In fact, it was Joy's opinion, based on some of the things John Doe said, that he hadn't seen Hannah for quite some time. Joy said he was anxious to get something really special."

"Did you tell Finn about Hannah?"

I nodded. "He said he'd look in to it. Of course now he's probably distracted by this bank robber thing. I wonder if Bruce Drysdale was on Madrona Island to rob our bank."

Cody shrugged. "Could be. Or it could be that he was on the island to hide out. We're fairly isolated from the mainland."

"And we're fairly close to Canada," I added. "If he was looking to get really gone he could come to Madrona, rent a private boat, and disappear once and for all."

"I guess that's a possibility as well."

I was pouring myself a second glass of wine when my phone rang. I looked at my caller ID.

"Hey, Tara. what's up?"

"I was thinking about taking some magazines and stuff over to John Doe. What room is he in?"

"Three fifteen. I'm not sure how late visiting hours are."

"I'm going there now and I don't plan to stay long. I was just sitting here alone, feeling sorry for myself, and it occurred to me that I hadn't had a chance to meet the man you've been trying to help."

"I'm sure he'll appreciate the company, but the nurse is something of a barracuda, so don't overstay the time limit she gives you."

"Thanks for the heads-up. I'll see you in the morning."

I turned and looked at Cody after hanging up. "Tara's going to take some magazines over to our trauma victim."

"Speaking of Tara, I might have an idea of how to solve the dilemma of your loan."

"Really? What?"

"It occurred to me that you might be able to get a new loan to pay off the old one."

"We only have thirty days. Less than thirty days, now. I don't see how we can do everything that would be required to get a commercial loan in under thirty days, especially with the holidays just around the corner. Besides, Tara looked in to refinancing a while back when interest rates went down, and apparently, we aren't eligible for a new loan. At least not for that amount of money. The initial loan was pushed through by the bank manager or we wouldn't have qualified for it either."

"You may be right and maybe a new loan won't work, but I have a couple of ideas I can follow up on. I can't promise anything, but I'm willing to try as long as you're open to the idea."

"Of course I'm open to the idea. I'm sure Tara will be too." I got up and began clearing the table. "If there's any way at all to save the bookstore we're all over it."

Cody came up behind me and slipped his arms around my waist. I leaned back into his warmth. "Don't worry. We'll figure it out."

I closed my eyes and willed the tears that were threatening to remain at bay. "I know. It's just really frustrating that all of this is happening now."

He kissed my neck.

"Do you want to decorate first or have dessert first?" I asked as I grasped for something other than giant loans to focus on.

"Actually," Cody turned me around and kissed me softly on the lips, "I had something else in mind."

Chapter 7

Wednesday, December 14

I couldn't have been more surprised if you dropped a house on my head when I arrived at Coffee Cat Books the next day to find John Doe sitting with Tara having coffee.

"What are you doing here? Did you find your memory?"

He laughed. "No, I didn't, but your lovely partner here managed to get me sprung from the hospital, so I'm going to help out at the bookstore to repay her."

I was sure I looked as confused as I felt. "Huh?"

"As I planned, I went to the hospital last night to drop off the magazines I'd bought for John. The nurse you warned me about was off-duty and the replacement didn't seem to care a bit about how long I stayed, so he and I ended up chatting for quite a while."

"John? Is that actually your name? You said you hadn't gotten your memory back."

"No, but the hospital and the sheriff's office have me down as John Doe, so I decided to go with it for now."

"I see." I glanced at Tara.

"John and I found we had a lot in common. It's so strange that he can't remember his name, but he remembers how to make coq au vin. Anyway, one thing led to another and I mentioned we were having a hard time finding someone to play Santa this year and he offered to do it if he managed to get out of the hospital in time. I spoke to Dr. Ryan first thing this morning, who spoke to Finn, and everyone agreed there was no reason for John to be in the hospital, so I offered him my spare room and gave him a job."

"He's going to be *living* with you?"

"Temporarily."

I gave Tara a meaningful look. "Do you think you can help me get the cats settled in the cat lounge?"

"Sure." Tara glanced at John. "I'll be back in a few minutes and we can continue our conversation."

As soon as we were outside I turned to Tara. "Are you crazy? You don't even know this guy."

"I know, but we talked for a long time last night and he seems really nice. Even you said he was charming and you wanted to help him."

"He has been charming and I do want to help him. He's probably a totally awesome person, but we don't know that. He could be a serial killer for all we know."

"He doesn't seem like a serial killer."

I took a deep breath and let it out slowly. "Does Finn know you had this guy move in with you?"

"No. Dr. Ryan called Finn to ask if there was any reason John couldn't be released. Finn said he wasn't under arrest, so if Dr. Ryan felt he was ready to be released and John wanted to be, there was no reason to keep him in the hospital. Dr. Ryan asked John if he had a place to stay and he said he did, so he signed the release papers."

I closed my eyes and shook my head. I was afraid my usually levelheaded friend had lost her mind. "I want to help John, but I can't let you do this."

"I'm an adult. I can make my own decisions," Tara insisted.

"I know that. I'm just worried."

"About what?"

"I'm worried this guy isn't really as charming as he seems and suddenly he'll remember that. I'm worried he actually *is* as charming as he seems and you'll fall in love with him, only to find out he's married when he gets his memory back."

"I'm not going to fall in love with him and we need a Santa."

"He has a bandage on his head and bruising on his face. He's going to make a pretty scary Santa."

"Santa has a hat, a full beard, and a mustache. All that will show are his eyes, and they're fine."

I opened my car door and reached in to gather the first of the four cats I'd brought with me that day. "How about if we let him play Santa but we find him somewhere else to stay?"

"Like where?"

"I don't know. Give me a couple of hours to work on it."

Although we hadn't planned to provide a Santa until Friday, and then only on the weekends, John would be a huge help in the store and the Santa suit would hide his injuries, so Tara dug out the costume we'd bought the previous year and Santa showed up at Coffee Cat Books that very day.

I still couldn't believe Tara had checked John out of the hospital, given him a job, and agreed to let him stay in her home.

I'm usually the rash one, while Tara is usually cautious and levelheaded. The entire situation made me wonder if John Doe was somehow hypnotizing people with his starling blue eyes.

I knew calling Finn to inform him of the current situation might bring down Tara's wrath, and I was more motivated than ever to find out who the man was now that he'd become a part of our lives. When I called his office I learned that Finn was in the field, responding to a residential fire. When he finally called me back I learned the fire appeared to have been arson involving a local contractor and the cookie-cutter houses he'd built. Finn was as shocked as I was that Tara had acted so uncharacteristically, but we both agreed that putting her on the defensive would only make her dig in her heels. The best course of action, we decided, was to keep an eye on things and find out the man's identity sooner rather than later. Finn, however, was going to be tied up sorting out details surrounding the fire, though he promised to follow up on a few leads as soon as he had the opportunity.

I considered the situation as I restocked shelves. I still had a couple of leads I hadn't had the time to follow up on myself. I remembered John had asked for the location of a jewelry store. If he'd purchased expensive jewelry from a local vendor perhaps he'd been forced to use a credit card.

"Cody and I still need to go over a few things before rehearsal tonight," I announced after the restocking was complete. "John is here to help you, so I thought we'd meet for an early lunch."

"That's fine," Tara said.

"I won't be too long. If it gets too crazy text me and I'll come back early."

I'd called Cody to tell him what I was doing. He was covering the fire and wouldn't be able to meet me as planned, and we agreed to meet for dinner before choir that night. I hoped to have news by the time we met so that we could figure out how to handle the new Santa in our lives.

Pelican Bay Jewelers was the closest of the stores to Coffee Cat Books, so I started there. The clerk on duty claimed not to have sold anything to a man fitting John's description, and I received a similar response from Rocks and Riches. O'Connell's Jewelry Store was in Harthaven, which was the reason I'd saved it for last.

"Mornin', June," I greeted the proprietor. We attended the same church, but I wouldn't say I knew the woman well. She did tend to be the suspicious sort, so I'd have to be careful how I asked my questions. Knowing her, if she thought I was up to something she'd refuse to answer on principle alone.

"Morning, Cait. What brings you in today? You aren't here to try to talk me into making the sauce for the spaghetti dinner, are you? Because I already told Father Kilian I couldn't do it this year."

"No, I'm not here on behalf of the church or the spaghetti feed committee. I'm here to ask about a man who may have been in here last weekend. He was in the bookstore and forgot his change, so I am trying to track him down to return it. He never told me his name, but he mentioned he wanted to buy a piece of jewelry and I told him to come to you."

"Thanks; I appreciate that. Word-of-mouth advertising makes all the difference to a small store like this one. What did he look like?"

I described John the best I could.

"Yeah, he was in. He was interested in a birthstone locket. He even wanted it engraved."

"Did he happen to give you his name or address?"

June pursed her lips as she considered my question. "I'm sure his name must be on the order form."

"Can you check, please? It's important. His change was actually a fairly substantial amount."

June opened a drawer that was located under the cash register and pulled out a file. She selected a small manila envelope and opened it. "Here we go. How odd. He didn't leave a name other than the one he wanted engraved on the locket."

"And what was that?"

"Hannah."

"Did he pay with a credit card?"

"Cash."

The fact that John Doe was running around town with a huge amount of cash seemed more than just a little suspicious to me. "Do you mind if I ask how much the locket cost?"

"Two hundred and fifty dollars plus tax. Why?"

"Just wondering. Thank you for your time. I'll try to track him down another way."

By the time I got back to the bookstore there was a long line of children waiting to see Santa. John greeted each child with a smile and a twinkle in his eye. He helped them onto his lap and then he took a minute to chat with each one before asking for their Christmas wish. The moms and dads who had brought their little darlings for a visit with Santa more often than not bought a drink and then browsed through the books while they waited. There was no doubt about it: John Doe was going to be good for our bottom line.

"How was lunch?" Tara asked.

"Good," I answered, even though I'd never gotten around to eating. "It looks like John has settled in."

"He's so good with the kids. Not that I expected him to be bad with them, but I wasn't expecting this. He takes the time to really connect with them. It's almost like he's the real Santa Claus."

Now that would be an interesting twist to his story.

I was about to mention the locket to Tara, but somehow I suspected she'd be mad that I'd been sleuthing behind her back. I was certain she still wanted John to find his identity, but based on the way I'd reacted this morning, she'd probably think I was investigating with the intention of interfering with the decision she'd made rather than to help him find the life he'd lost.

I grabbed my phone from my pocket and looked at it, pretending I had a text.

"It looks like Siobhan needs to speak to me," I improvised. "Do you think you and John can handle things for a while longer?"

Tara smiled. "John and I will be fine. He's been such a huge help."

"Okay, great. I shouldn't be long."

"Take your time."

I watched as Tara glanced at John with a twinkle in her eye. Yup, there was no doubt about it; Tara was mesmerized— or possible hypnotized.

I actually did head to Siobhan's office. I really wanted to sit down with Finn, or possibly Cody, to come up with some sort of alternate plan for John's lodging, but because they were both tied up, experience had shown that Siobhan was the next best thing.

"Tara asked him to move in with her?" Siobhan was as shocked as Finn and I had been.

"Temporarily. He seems like a nice enough guy, but we don't know a single thing about him. It makes me uneasy to think of him sleeping in her apartment. At least when he's at the store there are other people around."

"He's probably been on the island for almost a week. He must have been staying somewhere before he was hurt."

"A lot of people have said he mentioned he was staying in a cabin, but I checked with the three big rental agencies and none of them have admitted to knowing who he is."

"There are a lot of vacation home owners who handle their rentals themselves," Siobhan said, repeating something I already knew. "I have a list of the homes that are registered as vacation rentals, although there are quite a few landlords who operate outside the system. Is there a way we can narrow things down a bit?"

"I don't know. The people I spoke to just said he mentioned he was renting a cabin on the water."

"There are a lot of waterfront cabins on the island." Siobhan sighed. "I suppose trying to locate the cabin without additional information would be like looking for a needle in a haystack."

"Yeah. This whole thing seems so strange to me. John seems nice enough. Every single person I spoke to said he was charming and a good tipper. He seems to have purchased quite a few things during his first days on the island and in every instance he paid cash. In this day and age, when everyone has a credit or debit card, why would anyone carry around that much cash? It makes no sense."

"Maybe he'd suffered a bankruptcy at some point in the past and couldn't get a credit card?" Siobhan offered.

"If he did go through a bankruptcy he certainly bounced back. He has to have dropped a couple grand since he's been here."

"He might have been carrying cash if he didn't want to leave a paper trail. Maybe he's married and here with his lover, or maybe he's on the run for some reason."

Neither of those choices made me feel good about the fact that John was suddenly so firmly entrenched in Tara's life.

"Do you have any other leads you haven't followed up on yet?" Siobhan asked.

"No, I don't think so. I guess I could check with the guys who work the ferry to see if anyone remembers him. It's doubtful one man would stand out among the many who ride the ferry every day, but Marley said he had a blue Mercedes with paper plates, so it's possible the guys who work the car deck might remember something like that."

"If you knew for certain what day he arrived you'd at least have a starting point."

"It looks like all the purchases he made were last Saturday. If I had to guess I'd say he came in on the Friday ferry. Of course he could have arrived before that, but I haven't come across anyone who remembers seeing him prior to Saturday."

I leaned back in my chair and closed my eyes. This entire situation was giving me a headache. "There *is* one lead I haven't done anything with." I opened my eyes and sat forward. "Antonio told me that when John ate at his place he joined a family of seven. He mentioned he had an uncle who lived in Italy whose last name was Pizzano. I imagine there are a lot of Pizzanos in Italy, and Antonio didn't have any additional information that would help us narrow it down."

"Do you think John Doe's real last name could be Pizzano?"

"Maybe. But it just as easily might not be. We don't even know if he was referring to a real uncle or an honorary one."

"I suppose you could mention the name to John to see if he shows a reaction," Siobhan suggested.

"I guess it wouldn't hurt to try." I looked out the window. "It looks like it's going to rain again."

"Personally, I've been hoping for snow."

"Yeah, me too. The only thing I like about rain is the sound it makes when it hits the roof."

"There is something pleasant about that sound."

I frowned. "John said something to me about the sound of rain, now that I think of it."

"It's rained on and off for over a week," Siobhan pointed out.

"Yeah, but John specifically said that while he remembered the sound of rain, it wasn't raining."

"Maybe a drippy faucet?"

"I thought of that, but he said no. He also said it wasn't sprinklers or water dripping off a surface of some sort."

"There are those noise machines that provide an artificial rain sound, or maybe he was in a store that had a fountain."

"The cabin where he's staying could have a fountain."

Siobhan sat back in her chair with a look of contemplation on her face. Like me, Siobhan enjoyed a puzzle, and I could see the situation had her intrigued.

"You said John said he heard rain, but it wasn't raining. What about rocks?"

"Rocks?"

"The rocks on Black Rock Beach."

Siobhan had a point. Black Rock Beach was covered with smallish round rocks that were situated on a slope. When the tide came in it lifted the rocks that then feel back on each other as the water receded, causing a sound that very much resembled rain. Very loud rain.

"There are several cabins near that beach," I said.

"It wouldn't hurt to check."

"Do you have time?"

"I'll make time."

The road leading to the beach Siobhan had referred to ran parallel to the water, so all the homes on one side backed up to the sea. There were several cabins close enough to the rocks for their occupants to witness the high tide phenomenon, but by the process of elimination we narrowed the cabins John could have rented down to two. I still had the key from the wallet, so I walked up to the first cabin and knocked. When no one answered I tried the key. The door opened.

The cabin was newly remodeled, with a spectacular view. It was spotlessly clean and looked unlived in other than the pile of brightly wrapped gifts stacked under a tree that was adorned with a variety of Christmas decorations. There were stockings hanging on the mantel and I noticed a huge bouquet of red and white roses on the table. The smaller of the two bedrooms was decorated in a cream color that might have seemed almost too plain if not for the variety of stuffed animals stacked on the bed.

"You don't think John had a child with him?" Siobhan asked.

"Joy Holiday from Sullivan's told me John was there looking for a gift for a seven-year-old named Hannah. And I found out he also purchased a necklace for Hannah. I had the impression she wasn't with him. Joy didn't think he'd seen her for quite some time."

"Based on the look of things, it appears he was anticipating a visit."

"Yeah, it does look that way."

Siobhan went to check the kitchen while I walked into the second bedroom. It was a standard rental room: nice but not personalized in any way. I looked in the closet, which held nothing but clothing, and then began opening and closing dresser drawers, which, like the closet, held only clothing. I opened the drawer on the bedside table, where I found an envelope with a single sheet of paper tucked inside.

Dear T,

I know I agreed to give us a second chance after you assured me you had changed. However, now that the time has come, I find I've changed my mind. I'm not going to meet you on the island. I've filed for divorce, which, given the fact that we've been separated for two years, is long overdue.

Sincerely, R

The envelope must have been hand delivered, or perhaps it had come in another outer envelope because there wasn't a name, address, or postmark on the exterior of the one I held.

"Look what I found." Siobhan held up a half-empty bottle of whiskey.

"Yeah, well, read this and maybe the whiskey will make sense."

Chapter 8

Siobhan and I gave the letter to Finn, who was back in his office by the time we got back to town, in the hope that he could find some sort of physical evidence to help us discover John's identity. Siobhan used the address of the cabin to track down the owner, who told her he'd rented the cabin to a man who hadn't provided any personal information but had been willing to pay the full holiday rate for an entire month upfront. The owner had gone along with the unusual arrangement because, he said, the man seemed interested in finding a quiet place to escape the holiday hoopla.

"Do you think John was running from the law?" I asked Finn.

"I don't know."

"It seems odd that he had so much cash but never gave his name to anyone. I wasn't comfortable with John Doe staying with Tara when she first mentioned it, but now I'm feeling even worse."

"It seems he has a cabin he's paid for through the middle of January," Finn pointed out. "I can firmly suggest he stay in the cabin rather than with Tara."

"I'd feel better about that."

"Tara can't legally hire John Doe if he doesn't have ID or tax information," Siobhan pointed out.

"I don't think she's paying him. I think he was just volunteering at this point. I'm less concerned about that because there are people around in the store all the time. Do you think if you take John to the cabin it will jar his memory?" I asked.

"It's worth a try," Finn answered.

When we got to the store we decided to wait until Coffee Cat Books closed. There was a line of children out the door who weren't going to be happy if we took Santa away before the end of his shift. Plus, I wanted to do this as smoothly as possible so I wouldn't be upsetting Tara. When we told John we'd found the place he'd been staying before he was hurt he was anxious to pay a visit, hoping it would spark a memory.

Finn, Siobhan, Tara, and I all accompanied John to the cabin. When I'd explained the situation to Cody he'd agreed to go on ahead to choir practice to get things started. I was going to have to wait a while longer for the meal I still hadn't managed to eat that day.

John had a blank look on his face as we pulled up in front of the cabin. I watched him closely as he got out of the car and walked up the cement walkway to the front door. When I unlocked it using the key I'd found in the wallet he stepped inside. He looked around the room, but his expression didn't change at all.

"Does anything seem familiar?" Finn asked.

John shook his head.

"Why don't you go ahead and walk around?" Finn suggested. "Maybe something will come to you."

John walked from room to room, touching surfaces, picking up gifts. I could see by the lack of emotion on his face that nothing seemed any more familiar to him than the things we'd talked about in the hospital.

"You think I was staying here?" John asked. There was an obvious look of confusion on his face.

"We believe so," I answered. "For one thing, I found the necklace you bought for Hannah on the dining table. It's engraved, just like the one the man fitting your description bought on Saturday."

"Do you have the necklace?" John asked.

"It's still on the table. I'll get it."

I handed the necklace to John as he stared blankly at the clothes in the closet.

I swear I saw a flash of something on his face before it was masked and his blank stare set in.

"May," he said.

"May?" I asked.

"It's an emerald, the birthstone for May."

John carefully turned over the necklace and looked at the inscription. He ran his thumb over it but didn't say anything. He looked forlorn, though, as he looked around the room. My heart was breaking for him, and I could see Tara was fighting back tears.

"We should go," she suggested. "This is too much for him."

"No," John said. "I want to stay." He looked at Finn. "If that's okay."

"I think that would be fine," Finn answered.

"But..." Tara began.

He took her hand and looked deeply into her eyes. "Maybe if I stay I'll remember something."

"Will you come to the bookstore tomorrow?"

John looked at me. "Do I have a car?"

"We haven't been able to locate it," Finn said.

"I'll come pick you up," Tara offered. "Say nine?"

John looked around the room to locate a clock. "Nine is fine."

"Do you have food?" Tara asked.

Siobhan opened the fully stocked refrigerator.

"Okay, then I'll see you at nine," Tara agreed as I ushered her out.

Finn, Siobhan, and I debated whether we should give the note I'd found to John, but we decided to wait. We'd sprung enough on him for one day.

By the time I made it to choir practice, which this week was actually play rehearsal, Cody had everyone organized and in place.

I hurried over and took my place next to Cody. "Sorry I'm late."

"How'd it go?"

"I'll tell you later. What's up with Robby's costume? I thought he was going to be a sheep."

"He was, but he's insisting he won't be in the play unless he can wear the Batman cape he got for Halloween, so now he's Batsheep."

"If we let him be Batsheep we'll have a flock of superhero sheep before we know it."

"I thought of that, but the play is for the kids, so I really don't see the harm in a little improv. Last week Ricky and Robby wouldn't settle down and say their lines for anything and this week they've been serious and attentive and haven't missed a single line or cue."

"Ricky isn't a sheep. He's an angel," I pointed out.

"Yes, but now he's Super Angel."

I had to admit giving the kids a bit of freedom with their costumes and lines for the dress rehearsal made for a funny and heartfelt experience. It wasn't like we were going to perform during a service. The play was really meant for the kids and their families, so I supposed Cody was right; where was the harm in letting the kids add their own twists to the timeless story? I laughed and cried when Super Angel arrived at the manger and informed Mary in a quite serious tone of voice that our Lord and Savior was much too special to be born in a stable, so he was going to fly her to the nearby Holiday Inn, where his mom had a free upgrade.

"That was the most adorable telling of the Christmas story I've ever seen," I said to Cody as we headed toward Antonio's for dinner. "Although, having said that, I'm sort of afraid to see what they'll come up with for the actual performance."

"I think the kids will probably stick to the original script. They want to do a good job when their families are watching. I think tonight was just about them expressing what was in their hearts and minds."

"You know, you're going to be a wonderful father someday."

"Are you trying to tell me something?" Cody asked with a serious expression on his face.

"No, I'm not pregnant. It's just that when I see how good you are with the kids—even the difficult ones—I find myself looking ahead to how things could be and I hope someday will be."

Cody took my hand in his and gave it a squeeze.

Luckily, Antonio's wasn't too crowded at that time of the evening, so we managed to snag a table for two by the fire. There was a beautifully decorated tree in the corner and the sounds of Christmas piano playing on the stereo. It was quiet and romantic and exactly the sort of end of the day I needed after the hustle and bustle of the past few.

"It seems we never have gotten around to decorating your tree," Cody reminded me.

"I know. It's been such a crazy week. Maybe you could come over tomorrow after work. I'll even cook. Or at least reheat. I have leftovers in the freezer."

"Leftovers sound wonderful. I'll bring some wine."

"It would be nice if you could stay."

Cody placed his hand over mine. "I'd like that. I feel better about staying now that Mr. Parsons has Harland to keep him company."

"I'm glad the two of them are getting along so well. Given the fact that they're both ornery old coots, it could have gone either way."

"I made reservations for us for New Year's," Cody informed me.

"Where are we going?"

"Idaho. I found a quaint little cabin right on a small lake with miles of forest surrounding it."

"Isn't Idaho kind of far to drive for a few days?"

"Which is why we're flying. I found a charter company based on Orcas Island and Danny agreed to take us over to Orcas, so we don't even have to worry about the ferry."

"That sounds perfect. Better than perfect. It sounds magical."

Chapter 9

Wednesday, December 21

It had been a week since John had started work at Coffee Cat Books and we'd settled into a comfortable routine with him playing Santa by day and hanging out with Tara at night. He still hadn't remembered who he was, but it was obvious he was a kind man with a good heart. The kids who came to see him absolutely adored him, and it didn't take long for families from the other islands and even the mainland to make special trips to visit the magical Santa who seemed to be able to make every child he spoke to feel wanted and understood.

Somewhere along the way, Tara had shared the letter I'd found with John. He seemed confused and saddened by the fact that he'd apparently been estranged from his wife for two years. The fact that it appeared he had a child of his own in the world made him even more determined to regain his memory and find his identity. Tara had taken him around town to see all the people I had chatted with during those first days after he'd been injured, and while they all remembered speaking to him, he didn't seem to remember any of them.

Still, it didn't take long for the charming and personable man to make friends with practically everyone on the island. Tara asked him to play Santa at the St. Patrick's spaghetti dinner on Saturday night, and it was obvious based on the line of people who wanted to greet him that John Doe had found a home on Madrona Island whether he regained his memory or not.

I know I'd had my doubts when Tara brought him home like a stray puppy, but after watching him for a week all my doubts had been resolved. I think the moment he pitched in after dinner at my mom's on Sunday to tackle the cleaning up, after insisting Mom had done more than her share and deserved a break, I felt the last of my fears fade away.

And the fact that John was such a popular Santa had been great for our bottom line. The bookstore was busier than we'd ever dreamed it could be, and Tara was even talking about expanding our novelty inventory with some of the unexpected profit we'd managed to tuck away, if we were able to keep the store when we finally spoke with Anthony Princeton.

We weren't sure what had happened to the money John had had when he arrived on the island. He hadn't found any cash in the cabin. If he'd hidden it he naturally couldn't remember where. Not that it mattered much; Tara made sure to slip him a little cash each day, assuring me we'd square up with the IRS once John regained his memory, which she was confident would happen any day.

"That Santa you hired this year is a real gem," a woman who'd come over on the first ferry this morning whispered to me. "My Polly has always been scared to sit on Santa's lap. I'd pretty much given up on the idea of getting a photo this year, but look at her now."

I glanced at Santa, who was chatting with a dark-haired girl in a red dress who looked to be three or four.

"He does seem to have a way with kids," I agreed. "We had a woman come in yesterday with a little boy with social anxiety disorder. The boy looked like he was going to have a meltdown when he first arrived, but then Santa knelt in front of him and said something and he went straight into his arms. He didn't speak, but he sat on Santa's lap for close to fifteen minutes. His mom said that was the longest she'd ever seen him sit so quietly."

"I guess we'll need to start referring to him as the child whisperer."

"Yeah," I said, "I guess we will."

The midday ferry had just left the dock when I got a text from Finn, asking me to come by his office. Normally, if he had a question or needed some information from me he'd simply ask by text or call, so I was fairly certain whatever he wanted to talk about had something to do with our Santa.

"Finn has a few questions for me and asked me to stop by," I told Tara.

"Does he have news about John?"

"He didn't say. He probably just wants my opinion about a Christmas gift for Siobhan. It looks like you and John have things under control and the next ferry won't be here for three hours, so I think I'll head over now to see what's on his mind."

Tara straightened one of the bows on the tree we'd decorated with coffee cup, cat, and book ornaments. "That's fine. If he does have news about John let us know right away." Tara glanced at Santa, who was chatting with a child. "I think the not knowing is beginning to wear on him. He told me he's been having nightmares. In the beginning he figured he'd get his memory back after a few days, but now that it's been more than a week I think he's suspecting he may never remember who he is or, more importantly, who Hannah is."

"Has he remembered anything at all?"

"Yeah. Small things that don't seem to fit together. He isn't even sure the memories are real. Dr. Ryan told him there was a good chance everything would come flooding back in one giant wave at some point. I guess John's clinging to that hope, but I know he's getting more and more frustrated."

"If Finn has news I'll let you know right away," I promised.

I felt for John. If I suspected I had a child somewhere in the world but couldn't remember who she was or what had become of her, I'd be having nightmares as well.

I decided to walk down to Finn's office. It was only a few blocks and it had turned out to be a beautiful, sunny day. The rain had stopped and we never had gotten the snow I'd hoped for, but walking along the festively decorated Main Street on a crisp, cool day with brilliant sunshine and a gentle breeze wasn't too bad at all.

"You rang?" I teased as I walked into Finn's office. Siobhan and Cody were already there, and based on the solemn looks on their faces, the news I was about to receive probably couldn't be classified as good.

"What happened?" I asked when Finn didn't answer right away.

"We may have found John Doe's identity," he answered.

"Who is he?"

"Have a seat and I'll fill you in."

I did as Finn instructed.

"A body has been found in a shallow grave on the north shore," Finn began. "It appears the man has been dead for at least a week, maybe longer. The medical examiner was able to use dental records to identify him as Bruce Drysdale."

"The bank robber?" I asked.

"One and the same."

I waited. There wasn't much to say as I waited for the punch line.

"I've been looking into the bank robberies since Cody informed me that Mr. Drysdale had been seen on the island. Apparently, he didn't act alone."

Uh-oh. I could see where this was going.

"He had an accomplice who was never identified because he wore a mask he never removed, but he was described as being tall with dark hair and blue eyes. The eyes were visible through the holes of the mask, and one witness reported seeing dark hair sticking out at the spot where the mask met the collar of his shirt."

"And you think John was his accomplice?"

"We don't have any proof of it of course, but John is six feet two inches tall and he does have dark hair and blue eyes. He also showed up on Madrona Island with a whole lot of cash at around the same time we suspect Drysdale did."

I sat in silence. I'm not sure what I was expecting, but it wasn't this. John was such a sweet, charismatic guy. He seemed to have a magical way about him that didn't fit at all with the notion of him robbing banks.

"Do you think John came to the island with Drysdale and then killed him?" I choked out.

"It's a theory."

There had to be a mistake. I wanted to argue on John's behalf, but I thought of Tara and knew it was more important to be certain at this point rather than acting on gut instinct. Besides, the note I'd found made it sound as if the man it was intended for had recently promised to turn over a new leaf. Could John have been Drysdale's partner and might they have fought if John had told him he wanted out?

"So what are we going to do? How are we going to prove whether John is the man who helped rob the banks?"

"I don't know yet," Finn answered. "So far the police haven't been able to recover any physical evidence from the robbery sites or Mr. Drysdale's body that can help us identify the second man. The state police have retrieved video surveillance from the banks, but the second man was wearing a black ski mask and black clothing in every instance. He never speaks, allowing Drysdale to do all the talking, and so far, the forensic team hasn't been able to pick up any distinguishing characteristics other than blue eyes and dark hair."

"Are you going to arrest John?"

"I don't have probable cause to do so. Bringing him in for questioning won't do us any good either because he can't remember anything, and I already ran his prints, so we know that's a dead end."

"The second guy didn't leave any prints at all?"

"He wore gloves. Black leather gloves."

"Maybe we should search the cabin John is renting," I suggested. "If we find a black ski mask or black leather gloves maybe we can match them to the ones in the video."

"It seems like a long shot and I don't have enough to justify a warrant."

"I'll ask John if I can check his house for an earring I lost when we were there the other day. I doubt he'll have a problem with it, and while I'm there I'll look around to see what, if anything, I can find."

"Like I said, it's a long shot, but I suppose at this point it's all we have."

When I returned to the bookstore I lied, telling Tara Finn wanted my opinion on some earrings he had bought for Siobhan. I then segued into the fact that while I was with Finn I'd realized I'd lost one of my earrings at John's place and asked if it would be all right if I went there to look for it. He said it was fine and gave me the key. He really was the nicest guy and I hoped with all my heart he wasn't who Finn suspected he might be. Not only would Tara be crushed but I suspected John would be as well. Even if at one point he'd been a man who would rob banks and kill his partner, he most certainly wasn't that man now.

Cody didn't want me to go to John's house alone, just in case there was a third partner lurking around, so he locked up the newspaper office and went with me. It felt like a violation to search through John's closet and drawers, but if there was proof of his identity there, I was determined to find it.

"I feel like I have a hundred-pound weight on my heart," I said to him as I searched the closet while he pulled out dresser drawers.

"I feel the same way. As far as I'm concerned, John has earned the title *friend* in my book. Despite everything he must be feeling he's been nothing but kind and helpful. It's hard to imagine anyone with a gentler spirit than John has shown us this past week could ever have harmed another person."

I stood on tiptoe to reach a stack of boxes. "We don't know that he did. Other than the fact that he's the same height and coloring as the bank robber and that he came to the island with a lot of cash, we have no proof he's involved in the bank robberies in any way."

I set down the box and opened the lid. Inside was a hand-illustrated book entitled *Hannah's Christmas Adventure*.

"Look at this." I held up the book.

Cody came up behind me and looked over my shoulder as I read the story, about a little girl named Hannah who set off on an adventure to the North Pole to find Santa, who she suspected was her father. It seemed Hannah had learned she'd been adopted at an early age and she was sure, because of a birthmark on her shoulder shaped like a Christmas tree, that she was the daughter of Mr. and Mrs. Claus.

"This book is amazing." I slowly turned the pages. Each scene from the book was accompanied by a beautiful drawing that must have taken hours to complete.

"If John wrote and illustrated the book he could have it published," Cody agreed.

"It's too bad he didn't sign it. Of course if he created the book for Hannah and didn't intend to publish it, I guess there was no reason for him to."

Cody finished searching the cabin while I put the book back where I'd found it. We didn't find black gloves and a ski mask or bank bags full of money. I suppose the lack of these items didn't prove John wasn't the masked robber, but the lack of any results certainly didn't lend itself to the conclusion that John was the man the police were looking for.

The play had been performed the previous weekend and Cody and I had decided not to hold any choir practices until school resumed in January, which meant we had a rare Wednesday night off. I still hadn't completed my Christmas shopping and I never had gotten around to looking at the window displays, so we headed into town for dinner and to see where the night would take us.

"This scampi is so good," I gushed as I bit into one of the plump shrimp swimming in the most delicious sauce I'd ever eaten.

"My steak and lobster is really good too. I'm glad we finally got around to trying this place. I love the food at all the regular places we go, but it's nice to mix it up every now and then."

"I remember how delicious the seafood lasagna from Antonio's tasted the first time I tried it. I still love it, but there's something about experiencing a dish for the first time."

"Which very well may be the only benefit of memory loss," Cody mused.

"That's true. If your memory was wiped clean you could relive all your firsts. Your first kiss, the first time you read what turned out to be your favorite book, the first time you tasted chocolate…"

"Given the choice, I'd like to hang on to my memories, but I suppose there are a few firsts I wouldn't mind reliving."

"I suppose life would seem fresh and full of potential. If you could overcome all the fear and confusion that comes with losing your memory, of course."

"Yes, there is that."

"I think Tara is falling in love with John," I said in a much more somber tone of voice. "It's going to break her heart if he turns out to be a bad guy."

Cody didn't answer. He knew as well as I did that the chance of John being bank robber number two was huge, even if we didn't find anything to tie him to the robberies in the cabin. If it did turn out that in his past life John was this bad person, that would lend itself to an interesting discussion about the nature vs. nurture controversy. Could John have been born an inherently good man who had suffered some sort of hardship, changing the trajectory of his life forever? It was an interesting concept, but I hoped it wasn't true. What I wanted more than anything for Christmas this year was to wake up to find that John really was the man I'd come to know and love—in a platonic way of course—and not some monster who'd killed the man who had once been his partner in crime.

"Do you think we should get John a gift for Christmas?" I asked Cody. "At this point it looks like he'll still be on the island and I know Tara has invited him to Christmas Eve at Mr. Parsons's."

"I suppose it would be nice to get him something. Any ideas?"

"Not a one, but we can add him to our list."

"Where do you want to start?"

"I guess the sporting goods store. Danny left me a note with item numbers and prices of exactly what he wants, so that should be an easy gift to knock out."

We left the warmth of the restaurant to find the temperature had cooled down quite a bit. There were even snow flurries in the air. They weren't large enough or heavy enough to stick to the ground, but they did lend a festive atmosphere to the night. I slipped my hand into Cody's and willed myself to relax. There was nothing I could do to help either John or Tara tonight, but there was something I could do to make sure our evening was a memory Cody and I would cherish. I began to hum a popular carol as we walked along the beautifully decorated street, took every opportunity to give him a hug or a quick kiss on the lips, and pointed out every wonderfully decorated window with childlike abandon. At first I was simply playing a role in an attempt to leave my somber mood behind, but somewhere along the way I actually began to have fun.

"Let's bail on the shopping and go ice skating," Cody said.

"Ice skating?"

"I remember you used to ice skate as a child. They set up a rink in the park. It'll be fun."

"I'm not sure I remember how."

"I'm sure it'll come back to you once you get on the ice. It'll be like falling off a bike."

I laughed. "First of all, that's exactly what I'm afraid of, and second, I don't think that's the saying. Although," I stopped walking and looked up at the snow in the sky, "it does sound like fun. Do they rent skates?"

"They do."

I won't say ice skating with Cody was the *most* fun I'd ever had. It was loud and crowded and I spent most of the time on my backside, but skating hand in hand with Cody as Christmas carols played in the background and ten-year-old boys skated around us as they chased one another, turned out to be one of the most memorable moments I'd had in a very long time.

"Hot cocoa?" Cody asked after we left the rink to the actual kids.

"Add a splash of brandy and you have a deal."

"The bar it is, then. That was fun."

"My butt's going to disagree with you given all the times I landed on it, but yeah, it was fun. Maybe we should do it again some time. I bet with a little practice I could manage to stay on my feet."

"I think they plan to leave the rink up until after Valentine's Day. We should buy some skates while we're in the sporting goods store. It'll be easier if we have skates that fit our feet."

"I'm thinking about skipping the shopping portion of our evening altogether. I'm having a wonderful time, but suddenly I'm beat."

"How about we skip the shopping and the drink, buy some brandy, and head back to your place? I'll build us a fire, put on some music, make us some hot toddies, and rub all your sore parts."

"Cody, my love, you have yourself a deal."

Chapter 10

Thursday, December 22

I knew something was up when John didn't show up to work on time. Knowing what I did about the bank robberies and the dead man found in the shallow grave, I called Finn to see what was going on. It turned out the state police had shown up to interview John about the robberies. It seemed to me that interviewing a man who'd lost his memory was about as fruitless a task as any I could think of, and while Finn agreed, his hands were tied.

"How could they think John would do something like that?" Tara complained after I'd filled her in on the news I'd received the previous day.

"You and I both know John wouldn't hurt a fly, but we need to keep in mind that the person he was before he lost his memory and the one he is now might not be the same at all."

"Aren't you the one who told me how sweet and polite John was to everyone when he first arrived on the island?" Tara pointed out.

"Yes, I did, and yes, it does seem like he's a genuinely nice man."

"We need to help him," Tara said decisively.

"How can we do that?" I asked.

"We have to figure out who the second bank robber was and who really whacked the one who was buried on the north shore."

I supposed identifying the person who killed the man would go a long way toward clearing John, but I had no idea where to start and said as much to Tara.

"What about the cat? He's still hanging around, which, based on the behavior of the ones who have visited in the past, means he still has work to do. He hasn't done much at all since he found John on the beach. Maybe it's time to have a chat with him."

"I'm willing to try to find Drysdale's killer, but I'll need the day off."

"I'll call Cassie and have her come in." Tara looked me directly in the eye. "Please try to get to the bottom of whatever is going on. This is important."

I hugged her in response. "I'll do what I can. I promise."

Cassie was happy for the extra hours and agreed to come in right away, so I called Cody and let him know my plan before I headed home. I didn't have much to go on. I knew where Drysdale's body had been found and that he'd been involved in a series of bank robberies prior to his demise. I found a recent photo of him on the internet, which I supposed was as good a place as any to start. There wasn't much to go on, but if history was any indication, once I started asking around clues would present themselves.

I decided to start with Clarence.

"Okay, my little magical kitty, I need your help. This man," I held up the photo of Drysdale so the cat could see it, "was found dead on the north shore of Madrona Island yesterday. He was wanted in connection to a series of bank robberies that took place over the past couple of months. He had a partner who hasn't been identified but who resembles John Doe in terms of body build and coloring. If the man we now refer to as John is innocent we need to find the real killer and prove his innocence. And if he is guilty, I guess that's information we need as well. Understand?"

"Meow."

"Can you help me?"

Clarence jumped up onto my kitchen counter and knocked over the brandy bottle Cody had used to make toddies the previous evening.

"Brandy? You think I should nose around at the local bars?"

"Meow."

I guess that made sense. Cody had had a tip that Drysdale had been seen at Shots. There was also a bar just outside of Harthaven, Skullie's, that was pretty seedy. I personally didn't frequent the place because I liked my bars clean and friendly, but I knew Danny hung out there at times; it seemed to attract the fishing crowd. I called Danny and asked if he'd be willing to do some sleuthing with me. He wasn't busy, so he agreed.

I thanked Clarence, grabbed my keys, and headed to the marina to pick up my brother.

"I really appreciate this," I said after I'd filled him in on the situation.

"Happy to help. It gets boring this time of the year, when I don't have any tours going out. Are you sure the cat told you to start your search for this guy at Skullie's?"

"Clarence didn't actually tell me which bar to start with. In fact, all he really did was knock over a brandy bottle. For all I know, the person we're looking for is named Brandy, but I kind of think the bar lead will turn out to have more merit. I know Drysdale was seen at Shots, but they don't open for a couple more hours. Skullie's will be closed now as well, but I know you're friends with the bartender and hoped you'd be able to take me to his home."

"Yeah, I know where he lives, but if we're going to invade his space I'll do the talking."

"Deal. Which way do I go?"

"Hang a left at the entrance to the Harthaven Marina and follow the road to the second intersection. Turn left and his house is at the end of the dirt road."

I pulled up in front of the house and Danny turned to look at me. "Wait in the car. This shouldn't take long."

I handed Danny a photo of Drysdale, as well as one of John. I watched as Danny lumbered up to the front door. He knocked, and a man wearing only a pair of pants answered. Danny said something and handed him the photos. The man said something in return. Danny thanked him, then headed back to the car.

"What'd he say?"

"He said he'd never seen John before and was sure he hadn't been in, but he had seen the other man hanging around the bar. Drysdale showed up a couple of weeks ago, and he's pretty sure the last time he saw him was the Saturday night before last. He said he came in late and was already drunk when he showed up."

I remembered that Cody's informant had said Drysdale had been seen at Shots on both Saturday and Sunday. He must have headed over to Skullie's on Saturday night after he finished drinking at Shots.

"Did the bartender say whether he knew where Drysdale was staying or if he was with anyone at the bar?"

"He said Drysdale seemed to have a lot of cash to throw around, which meant he was a pretty popular guy on the island. He didn't know where he was staying, but Drysdale was seen leaving the bar a couple of times with a woman who's known to hang out with men who have money to spend."

"She's a hooker?"

"I don't think that's the way she would think of herself. She just likes nice things and dates men who will provide them. Her name's Vee."

"Do you know where to find her?"

"I do, and no, we haven't dated."

Danny did seem to date a lot of women, and at times I gave him a hard time about it, but even I wouldn't suggest that he'd date a woman like that.

"So where do we find her?"

"I know where she lives. Just take the road back into Harthaven. She lives in the apartment complex that backs up to the alley on First Street."

When we arrived at Vee's house, Danny once again suggested I wait in the car; he was likely to get more information out of her if he was alone. Harthaven is a small island village, not a large town, so I wouldn't say this was a bad neighborhood exactly, but the apartment complex where Vee lived was old and rundown and— because of the low rents, I assumed— tended to attract a less than ideal resident.

I hoped Danny would hurry. Sitting alone in the car in the alley behind the building gave me a feeling of discomfort, although I'd never had any dealings with the residents of this complex to suggest they weren't perfectly nice people who were simply down on their luck. I guess I'd had a pretty isolated upbringing that hadn't prepared me for the full spectrum of human existence.

"You know this is a no-parking zone," a young woman who was clearly with child informed me after tapping on my window.

"I know. I'm just waiting for my brother. He won't be long and I can move if I need to. Do I know you? You look familiar, but I can't quite place you."

"Tawny Grant. We went to high school together."

"Of course; I remember now. I'm sorry I didn't recognize you." The girl I remembered had long blond hair and dressed conservatively, while this woman's hair was jet black and she had a nose ring and a number of colorful tattoos.

"I change my look after my parents kicked me out."

I suddenly remembered that Tawny had been kicked out of the family home when she refused to break up with the musician she'd been dating. I glanced at Tawny's big belly. "Are you and Dingo still together?"

"No. He split when he found out he was going to be a daddy. It's just me now." Tawny rubbed her belly.

"Do you live in this building?"

"For now. I was laid off from my waitress job when I started to show. I guess a prego cocktail waitress isn't the image a bar like Skullie's is going for. You don't know of anyone who would be willing to hire someone who's seven months pregnant, do you? If I can't come up with the rent by the end of the month Guido and I will be out on the street."

"You're going to name your baby Guido?"

Tawny smiled. "No, it's just a nickname."

"I don't know if you heard, but Tara and I opened a bookstore. Coffee Cat Books. We might be looking for part-time help, if you're interested." If Tara could bring home a stray puppy on a whim so could I. "It's kind of far to travel if you don't have a car, but we could probably work something out."

The girl looked interested but didn't reply right away.

"Tawny," Danny greeted her on his return to the car. "I was wondering what happened to you."

"Got canned."

Danny frowned. "How's Guido?"

Tawny shrugged. "Okay, I guess. I've been kind of stressed out and the doctor said that isn't good for the baby, but it's hard to relax when you don't have a job or any way to pay your rent."

"Maybe I can help," Danny offered.

"Your sister just offered me a job."

Danny looked shocked. "She did?"

"I did," I spoke up. "How about if I pick you up here in the morning? Say nine-thirty? We can talk to Tara, but I'm sure we can work something out."

Danny chatted with Tawny for a few more minutes and then slid into the passenger seat of my car.

"You know Tara's going to flip if you bring someone who looks like her into your store."

"Maybe not. Tara has a soft spot for expectant mothers. Remember how she latched on to Destiny despite the brash attitude she had at the time? Tawny might not have the look of the usual Coffee Cat Books employee, but she seems nice enough. She was smart and hardworking when we were in school. At least she was until she met Dingo. If we can work out something I thought I'd take her shopping and buy her a few outfits that won't blow Tara's mind."

"Let me take her today. Before she talks to Tara," Danny offered.

"You hate to shop."

"Yeah, but I like Tawny. I want to help her. We know each other and I think she'll listen to me."

I shrugged. "If you want to."

"Take me back to get my car and I'll work out the details with Tawny. I'll even pick her up and bring her in for the interview. Say ten o'clock tomorrow?"

"I thought you were going to help me sleuth."

"I did. And I even got a lead. You can follow up from here."

I was more than just a little surprised at Danny's enthusiasm for helping Tawny. Not that he wasn't a nice guy, but he tended to put himself first a lot of the time, and volunteering to spend a day shopping with a girl who as far as I knew he barely knew wasn't a Danny sort of thing to do at all.

At least he really had managed to come up with a lead. Vee had told him that Drysdale had planned to go to Harthaven Marina on Saturday to talk to a man named Vinny about renting a boat. I didn't know Vinny well, but our brother Aiden docked his boat there and I was aware that Vinny owned several private vessels he rented out to affluent vacationers looking to tool around when they were on the island.

Vee had also said he'd made a comment about coming to the island alone but planning to meet a friend on Sunday. That would have been the day before I found John on the beach. My stomach knotted as I began to consider whether sweet, lovable John wasn't so sweet and lovable after all.

Vinny wasn't at the marina when I arrived, but the man working in the office gave me his phone number. When I called him, he informed me that he'd met with a man on Saturday, December 10, about a long-term rental on a yacht, but he'd needed to speak to his partner before committing. Drysdale was supposed to get back to Vinny the following day, but he never showed. I asked Vinny if Drysdale had mentioned the name of his partner; he'd never given his full name, but he'd said something about a Turner.

I sat in the car, staring out of the window, as I remembered the note we'd found in John Doe's cabin. It had been addressed to T. Could T stand for Turner? The more I dug into the events leading up to Drysdale's death and John's presence on the beach, the more convinced I was that John might be the criminal the police were looking for.

The only other thing Vinny had shared was that Drysdale had mentioned he'd gotten hammered the night before on fuzzy rum shots. They were basically just large shots of beer and rum, but as far as I knew there only one bar on the island that sold them: O'Malley's, a Hart sibling favorite. Aiden used to date the bar owner, Molly O'Malley, so I was certain if

Drysdale had been in and Molly knew anything about his movements in the days prior to his death, she'd be happy to tell me what she knew.

Unlike Skullie's, which was a total dive, O'Malley's was a family bar where many of the locals gathered to share a meal, have a drink, and discuss the local news. Molly had inherited the bar from her father when he passed away and as far as I could tell rarely took a night off. I guess I understood her need to keep an eye on things. The bar had been in her family since before she was born and the building as well as the regulars were like family to her.

O'Malley's served lunch and dinner, so it opened earlier than other places that just catered to the drinking crowd. I arrived there just after the midday lunch crowd had cleared out, so I sat at the bar to chat with Molly while I nibbled on my ham sandwich and diet soda.

"Aren't you usually working at this time of day?" Molly asked.

"I'm taking a day off to track down these two men." I pushed the photos across the bar. "Do you recognize them?"

"I don't recognize the cute guy, but I've seen the older one. He was in a couple of weeks ago. Why are you looking for them?"

"The older man is dead, so I'm not looking for him, but I am looking into his movements during the days leading up to his death."

"How many murders have you solved anyway?"

"A few. So, what can you tell me about the guy in this photo?"

"Nothing much. He sat at the booth in the corner and downed more fuzzy rums than any man should. I thought I was going to have to take his car keys, but a woman came by to pick him up just before closing."

"A woman? What woman?"

"I didn't know her. I don't think she lives on the island. I suppose she might have come to the island with him. It almost seemed like she was a wife or a girlfriend."

"Why do you say that?"

"She yelled at him when she got here. Called him a no-good lowlife. Typical things I hear on a regular basis from women whose husbands or boyfriends lose track of time and forget to come home."

"Did he come in again after that night?"

"Yeah. Once or twice. It seemed like he was a pretty big drinker. A few people I know from other bars mentioned he'd dropped a bankroll there as well."

"You said he left with a woman on one occasion, but did he always come in alone?"

"Not the last time. The last time he came in with a guy who was a good ten years younger than he appeared to be."

"Are you sure it wasn't the man in the other photo?"

Molly looked at the photo again. "No. That guy had similar coloring, but the one in your photo is much better-looking and had longer hair."

"Did you catch the younger man's name?"

Molly screwed up her face as she appeared to be considering my question. "Turner. The older guy in the photo you showed me called the younger man Turner."

So if Drysdale's partner was named Turner and Turner wasn't the man we knew as John Doe, maybe John really didn't have anything to do with Drysdale and his string of robberies. On the other hand, maybe the guy who met Drysdale wasn't his partner.

By the time I left O'Malley's Shots was open. It was early for the crowd the bar attracted so it was all but deserted. I walked up to the bar and ordered a diet cola. The bartender just stared at me.

"Don't have soda," he informed me.

"Wine?"

"Nope?"

"Okay, look, all I really need is information." I pushed the photos across the bar. "Do you recognize either of these men?"

"Yep."

"Which one?"

"Both."

"Do you happen to know their names?"

"Didn't ask."

"Okay; can you tell me when they were in last?"

The bartender paused. I thought he was considering my question, but then I noticed he was rubbing two fingers together, as if to let me know the information was going to cost me. I slipped him a twenty.

"The older guy was in a couple of times. The younger guy only once."

"And when was that?"

"Two weeks ago Sunday. I only remember that because the older man got into an argument with some of the other patrons about the playoff right in the middle of the Sunday-night game."

"And the younger guy was in at that time?"

"He was."

"Were the two men together?"

"No. The older guy came in first with another man. They sat in the corner. The younger guy in the photo came in later. He was already pretty smashed and sat at the bar. He looked like a man who had a problem that needed drowning. He also had a pile of cash, so he generously bought a round for everyone in the place."

"Did he say what his problem was?"

"No, and I didn't ask. I've been doing this for a long time. I can recognize the different types of drunk. There are those who are celebrating, those who struggle with addiction, those who're simply out to party, and those who're trying to drown a problem or a heartache. That man obviously fell into the last category."

"Did the two men talk?"

"Nope. The younger guy bought a couple of rounds and left."

"And the older guy?"

"Left shortly after that."

I wondered if Drysdale had followed John out of the bar. Drysdale was a thief and John was seen throwing around a bunch of money. I had to wonder if Drysdale had gone after John with the intention of mugging him. And if so, how did Drysdale end up dead and buried on the north shore while John turned up half dead just a half mile from the bar via the beach road?

When I returned to the bookstore John had a line of kids to see Santa. Tara informed me that the state police had released him after they'd questioned him, but they'd made it clear he was a person of interest and made him promise not to leave the island. John had agreed, and I was sure the police must have given his photo to ferry personnel as well.

I filled Tara in on the day's sleuthing the best I could between customers. I even mentioned that I'd run into Tawny and wanted to help her. Tara agreed we should help the poor girl, although she hadn't seen the new Tawny yet. I just hoped Danny was successful in getting her cleaned up a bit.

Chapter 11

I decided to stop by to chat with Finn. I hadn't learned a lot that day, but I had learned something, and maybe Finn had new clues or information as well. Finn's office was right next door to the newspaper, so once I'd chatted with Finn I'd see if Cody wanted to get together that night. I figured my best bet at carving out couple time was to combine sleuthing with dating.

"I was just about to call you," Finn said the minute I walked through the door.

"You have news?"

"I do, and it isn't the good kind."

I let out a long breath. "What now?"

"I found a car matching the description Marley gave you regarding the one driven by John Doe when he was at the Christmas tree lot twelve days ago. It was abandoned in the woods less than a quarter mile from the location where Bruce Drysdale's body was found."

I really didn't want to hear the rest of what Finn had to say. The fact that John's car was found near the murder scene couldn't be good.

"There were fingerprints all over the driver's area matching the ones I took from John at the hospital."

"It was his car. Or at least the one he was driving."

"There was also blood in the trunk. We're testing it as we speak, but I'm going to go out on a limb and assume the blood was Drysdale's."

"Are you going to arrest John?"

"If the blood comes back as a match, then yeah; I won't have a choice."

I hated it when things weren't coming together the way I'd hoped.

"If the car did belong to John, and he did indeed kill Drysdale and then dump the body, how did he get from the north shore, where the murder was committed, to the south shore, where I found him on the beach?"

"I don't know," Finn admitted. "Maybe he got a ride or perhaps he didn't act alone. I know Tara has developed a thing for him and I know it will devastate her if he turns out to be a bank robber and a killer, but I won't have much say in what happens if the state police get physical evidence that John killed Drysdale."

"I know. And thanks for the heads-up."

"You can't say anything to either John or Tara."

"I know."

"Uh, Cait, there's more," Finn added as I turned to go.

This couldn't be good. "More?"

"The car John Doe was driving was leased to Princeton Enterprises."

"As in the Princeton Enterprises that's trying to put Coffee Cat Books out of business?"

"I'm afraid so. I sent a photo to the human resources department. The person I spoke to had been there for less than a year, but she was sure she didn't recognize John and said he didn't work for the company. I have a message in to Anthony Princeton, but I was told he still wasn't reachable until after the holidays."

"Maybe if I talk to John about Princeton Enterprises he'll remember who he is and why he's here."

Finn shrugged. "Maybe. I'd tread lightly and let the memory come naturally."

I left Finn's office and headed next door to see if Cody was in. Luckily, he was. I felt like someone had just stabbed me in the gut. During the past week I'd gotten to know John, and the better I got to know him, the more certain I was that he was a kind and gentle man. I didn't have an explanation as to what might have happened to him, but I knew in my heart that the man everyone was calling the "real Santa" couldn't have killed anyone, and I was having a hard time believing he was on the island to evict us either, although that made more sense.

"What a nice surprise," Cody greeted me.

"I was next door talking to Finn. I'm afraid things aren't looking good for John." I shared the information Finn had passed on regarding John's car.

Cody frowned. "It does seem like evidence is piling up against him. Did Finn say how long it would be before they got the results of the blood test?"

"No. Probably a couple of days, but with the holiday this weekend who knows? What are we going to do? If he is guilty of killing Drysdale he definitely shouldn't be around a bunch of kids. But if he's innocent, we'll upset a lot of people for nothing if we pull him out of the store."

"If it's even a possibility that he killed Drysdale, I think you need to keep him away from kids."

"Yeah." I sighed. "I guess you're right. I'll pull Tara aside and fill her in. This is going to crush her."

"I know. But it's the right thing to do."

I looked at the clock. "Santa's shift will be over in another hour."

"Rather than pulling him out now, when there are kids around who have most likely been waiting for quite a while, why don't you just keep an eye on the situation until his shift is over and then have a chat with him?"

"It's not like he's going to suddenly get his memory back and start shooting people. Right?"

"I think that scenario is unlikely. Besides, he doesn't have a weapon. I'll come with you and we'll both keep an eye on things."

"Cody, there's more." I told him about John's car being leased to Princeton Enterprises.

We arrived at the bookstore a few minutes later only to confirm our suspicion had been correct; there was a line out the door and kids probably had been waiting thirty minutes or more. Cody made himself busy restocking shelves while I helped Tara at the coffee bar. I didn't want to get into things with her quite yet, so I just told her Cody had finished the work he needed to do for the day and decided to help us out. He'd done that before, so Tara didn't stop to question my explanation.

Cody and I had agreed to ease into the subject of Princeton Enterprises to see if John remembered anything on his own. We felt that way he might be more inclined to share whatever he knew.

John's shift ended up running longer than anticipated because we didn't want to send away kids who had been waiting so long. As it turned out, it was time for the store to close by the time we managed to free him up.

"I'll change out of this suit and help you clean up," John offered. "Quite a crowd today."

"I'm pretty sure we set a record," Tara agreed. "Maybe if Christmas was pushed back a month we'd make enough to pay off Anthony Princeton."

John froze.

I'd been struggling with a way to bring up the whole Princeton Enterprises thing, but it looked like Tara had just done it for me.

"Princeton?" John finally asked after a long pause. His face revealed his changing emotions. I felt as if I could almost see the memories begin to return.

Tara briefly explained about our loan and the complicated predicament we'd found ourselves in with the new owner. John appeared to be listening but didn't respond as he stood in the middle of the store, staring blankly as a range of emotions danced across his face. It was almost as if he was suddenly uncertain as to where he was. He closed his eyes and put his hands on either side of his head as if he were afraid it would fall off.

"Are you okay?" Tara asked.

"Tanner," John said. "My name is Tanner."

"You remember?" Tara smiled.

John frowned. "Not everything. Not much, actually. When you said the name Princeton it triggered one memory that led to another. They're fragmented. I can sense them, but they don't seem to fit together. It's as if—Oh, God." John closed his eyes again. He shook his head, as if to shake the memories free. He really did appear to be in both emotional and physical pain.

"Is your last name Princeton?" Tara asked. "Or did you attend Princeton University?"

Cody suggested that we put out the Closed sign and lock the door so no last-minute shoppers wandered in. Then we all took seats in the cat lounge. I thought John—or I guess I should say Tanner—looked as if he was going to pass out at any minute. Now that a door had been opened to his memory maybe we could find a way to help him recapture the past he seemed to have forgotten.

"Try to relax," Cody urged. "Take your time and let the memories come to you. Don't try to force anything. I'm not an expert, but it seems stress might have the opposite effect."

"My name is Tanner Woodson. I have a wife named Roxanne and a daughter named Hannah. I haven't seen either of them in two years."

We all sat in silence, allowing Tanner to work things out in his own time.

"I came to the island in the hope of making a fresh start."

A tear slipped down Tanner's cheek. Tara started to get up, but I motioned for her to wait.

"You mentioned a wife…?" I coaxed.

"Roxanne," Tanner answered.

"And you haven't seen her in two years," I added. "Are you divorced?" I remembered the letter and knew he wasn't, at least not yet."

Tanner looked to be in shock. He stared blankly into space.

"Take your time," Tara encouraged. "Just share with us what you remember as you remember it. Maybe try starting at the beginning and working your way forward."

Tanner looked at Tara. He smiled a sad little smile before he began to speak in a voice so soft I could barely hear him. "Roxanne left me because I wasn't as successful as she hoped I'd be. We met at a party after I began working for her brother, and despite the fact that we have very different personalities we hit it off. I'm not sure we would have stayed together in the long run, but Roxanne became pregnant with Hannah and we decided to try to make a go of it for the sake of our child. Roxanne talked her brother into giving me a promotion and a big raise, and for a while I made it work. But the pressure began to be too much for me. My performance slipped. I tried to tell Roxanne that I wanted to pursue a less stressful career, but she wouldn't hear of it. She wanted the lifestyle that only a high-powered position would support, and as her husband it was my responsibility to provide that. I tried to make it work; I really did. But in the end I gave up and quit my job. The day I told Roxanne about it was the last time I saw either her or Hannah."

"But you're Hannah's father," Tara pointed out. "You must have rights."

Tanner looked as if he was in physical pain. "Toward the end, when I was trying to make the career Roxanne wanted me to have work, I turned to alcohol. I'm not proud to admit I drank a lot more than anyone ever should. I made some mistakes." Tanner paused. "A lot of them. By the time I finally quit the job that was killing me Roxanne had enough on me to gain full custody. Instead of staying to fight I took the coward's way out and lost myself in a bottle."

By this point Tanner and Tara were both crying.

"And now?" I asked.

Tanner looked at Tara and me. I could see the apology on his face. I had a feeling we weren't going to like whatever he was about to say.

"Five months ago I ran into Roxanne's brother while he was on his way to a business meeting. I was sitting on a park bench, drunk as a skunk despite the fact that it was only ten o'clock in the morning. When he saw me he stopped and sat down next to me. He asked me how I'd been, and I think I made some sort of a rude reply. I never liked him. He's rich and successful; basically, everything I'm not. Everything Roxanne wanted me to be. Still, he took the time that morning to sit and chat with me. I was both touched and amazed when he called his secretary and told her that he wasn't going to make his appointment and asked her to rebook it. During the next couple of hours I found myself sharing everything that had happened to me and everything I'd gone through, not just since Roxanne had left me but since the moment I met her and she began the task of remaking me. This wonderful, caring man admitted he knew I wasn't cut out for the job his sister insisted I have, but he'd never been good at saying no to her. He wasn't surprised I wasn't happy or successful and he admitted he'd looked back on the decisions he'd made and admitted he owned a piece of everything that had happened."

"He sounds like a nice man," I said when Tanner paused.

"He is. At some point during the conversation Tony offered to pay for a hotel room for me. He gave me a fist full of money and encouraged me to attend AA and get myself cleaned up. I did as he suggested and that very night I vowed to turn my life around. Before meeting Roxanne I'd wanted to be a chef. I love to cook and I'd only taken a job with Tony's company in the first place so I could pay for culinary school. I didn't have a job, credit, or money, so Tony paid for me to get an apartment and helped me find a job working in a restaurant. I guess I was somewhat content with the way things were going, but I missed Hannah, and in a twisted sort of way, I even missed Roxanne. I mentioned that to Tony and he offered to help in any way he could. He arranged for Roxanne to bring Hannah to the island so we could try to rebuild our relationship and gave me a whole lot of cash so I could wine and dine her in the way she'd expect."

"So you went around town buying things you thought would make Roxanne and Hannah happy," I postulated.

"Yes."

"And then you got the letter," Tara supplied.

"Yes. Roxanne doesn't want to be married to a chef, even one who owns his own restaurant. She's filed for a divorce."

"You own your own restaurant?" Tara asked.

"Sort of. Tony bought me a building and promised to supply the start-up capital." Tanner looked around the room. "Tony bought me this building."

The room became totally silent. I'd suspected what was coming, but Tara hadn't. I could see she was shocked.

"This building?" Tara whispered.

"You're Anthony Princeton's brother-in-law," I stated.

Tanner glanced in my direction before looking back to Tara. "I'm sorry. I wasn't trying to hurt you. Or anyone. I needed a fresh start and Tony offered to help me. I really needed a way to try to get my family back and I honestly never thought about the fact that whoever was at the other end of the loan Tony purchased would get hurt."

"And now?" Tara asked.

"And now I do know, and as soon as I can gather my thoughts, I'm going to call Tony to tell him to call off the eviction. The store the two of you have built is so much more than any restaurant I could open. You've created a space filled with heart. I won't take it away from you."

Tara got up and crossed the room. She sat down next to Tanner, who was still dressed like Santa, and gave him a very inappropriate kiss, given the character he was dressed to portray.

"I'm so very sorry about your family," I offered. "Especially Hannah."

Tony smiled sadly. "I'll get her back. Maybe not full time, but for visitation. I'll need to find a job, and I'm not so sure Tony will be willing to help me out again after everything he's already done for me, but I'll push through and find a way."

Cody and I slipped out after the conversation shifted. It seemed obvious we had become little more than spectators.

"Do you think Anthony Princeton will let us keep the store?" I asked after we'd settled into Cody's truck.

"I don't know. There's still the very real fact that he owns the note and has the right to the due-on-demand clause, and there's also the fact that we still haven't explained how it is that Tanner's car appears to have been used in Drysdale's murder.

"I guess now that Tanner has his memory back we should just ask him what happened on the night he was left for dead on the beach. I'll text Tara to let her know we need to ask Tanner some additional questions. I'll suggest she bring him to the cabin for dinner. We can pick up something on the way home. Maybe by the time the night is over we can wrap up this mystery and get on with our holiday."

Chapter 12

Friday, December 23

"Okay, tell me in your own words what occurred on the evening of December 11," Finn said to Tanner the next day.

Danny had cleaned Tawny up and brought her into the store as promised and Tara had agreed to hire her on the spot. Tawny was willing to start right away, so Cassie and Tawny were holding down the fort while Cody, Siobhan, Tara, and I were watching from behind a one-way mirror while Finn took Tanner's official statement.

"Where exactly do you want me to start?" Tanner asked. I could see he was nervous. I couldn't blame him. He'd finally regained his memory after more than a week of not knowing who he was, only to find he was a suspect in a murder investigation.

"Let's start with the reason you're on Madrona Island, followed by the events of Sunday, December 11."

Tanner took a deep breath before he began. He looked around the room, as if trying to find something or someone. I wondered if he suspected we were watching.

"I came to Madrona Island on December 8 with plans to meet my wife and daughter, who I hadn't seen in two years. They were due to arrive on the midday ferry on Sunday, December 11. I arrived at the terminal just as the ferry was pulling up to the dock. A man who worked on the car deck met me at the debarking point and asked if I was Tanner Woodson. I said I was and he handed me a letter he claimed had been given to him by a woman at the port at Anacortes."

"And the contents of the letter?"

"It stated that my wife had changed her mind and wasn't going to meet me as planned. She told me that she'd filed for divorce."

"And what did you do at that point?" Finn asked.

"I stopped off at the liquor store, bought a bottle of whiskey, and went back to the cabin I had decorated for my family to drink it."

"And did you remain at the cabin for the remainder of the night?"

"No," Tanner answered. He looked down at his hands, which were crossed on the table in front of him. I could see he was struggling and I felt bad for him, but I knew it was important for Finn to know everything if he was going to be able to help him. "I'd been sober for long enough to know how really good it felt." He paused and looked up. "Somehow drinking my sorrows away by myself wasn't as comforting as it once had been. I decided to go into town and drink in a bar, where at least there were other people around for company. I ended up at Shots."

"Did you meet anyone at Shots?"

"No. I arrived alone and sat at the bar. I bought a couple of rounds for the crowd and then left. A tall man with dark hair, who I had seen sitting at a table in the corner with an older man, followed me out. When I arrived at my car he pulled a gun on me and demanded that I give him all my cash, my credit cards, which I didn't have, and the keys to my car. I complied. I thought he would leave with my cash and car, but instead he lifted his arm and pointed the gun at my head. I really thought I was dead."

"And then..." Finn encouraged.

"The older man from the bar came out. When he saw what was going on he called the man with the gun an idiot. He said something about not wanting to do anything that might get the cops involved. The man with the gun turned and shot the older man. I used the diversion to sneak away. I hid in the forested area across from the bar and watched as the younger man put the body of the man he'd shot in the trunk of my car and drove away."

"Was there anyone else in the parking lot when the man was shot?"

"No, not that I saw."

"And did anyone come out of the bar afterward?"

Tanner frowned. "Yeah, there was someone. All I can remember is that I saw a man near the door watching as the shooter drove away. I'm not sure if he'd heard the shot and had come to investigate of if he'd simply been leaving the bar and happened to come out at the exact moment the shooter pulled out of the lot."

"Do you think he saw the car leave the parking area?"

"Yes. He must have."

Finn jotted down a few notes, then asked, "Did anyone else come out of the bar?"

"Not that I saw. It's odd that the man didn't notify someone about the shooting,"

Tanner realized. "He must have come out after the body was already hidden away in the trunk."

"And what did you do at that point?"

"I wandered down to the beach. I was drunk and depressed. My cash and the car my brother-in-law had given me were gone. I felt like I had no reason to live, so I decided to kill myself. My plan was to swim out into the ocean until I drowned. I guess I must have walked down the beach as I tried to build up my courage. I honestly don't know how I ended up where I did. If I had to guess I'd say I passed out at some point and hit my head on the way down. The next thing I knew Cait was standing over me and I couldn't remember a thing." Tanner looked at Finn. "Am I going to jail?"

"It depends. If we can prove that things happened the way you claim, then no; you haven't broken any laws. The problem we have at this point is that all we have as proof of your innocence is your word. I'm not sure how that will hold up in court, if we even get that far, against the physical evidence that includes the car with your fingerprints on the steering wheel and Drysdale's blood in the trunk. To make matters even worse, your fingerprints were the only ones we found on the steering wheel."

"It was a brand-new car. I picked it up from the dealership just before I came to the island. Someone must have driven it off the truck and into the lot, and it must have been detailed before I arrived. I can't explain why the other man's prints weren't on the wheel. I guess that doesn't make sense."

"Did you notice if he was wearing gloves?"

Tanner closed his eyes, as if trying to bring the memory into more clarity. "Maybe. It was dark and I was drunk. It does seem that he might have had gloves on, now that you suggest it. Black. I think the man had on black gloves. They weren't bulky, though. They could have been made of nylon."

"Is there anything else you can remember?"

"No."

Finn pushed three photos across the table. "Are any of these the man who robbed you?"

Tanner picked up the photo and looked at it. "Yes. This one. This is the man who stole my money and my car and then shot the other man."

Finn pushed another set of photos across the table. "Are any of these the man you saw being shot?"

Tanner pointed to the photo in the middle. "This man. This is the man I saw that night."

"The men you've identified are Bruce Drysdale and Turner Carson. We know Drysdale was seen on the island with someone he referred to as Turner. I spoke to one of the investigators from the state police this morning who informed me that they've uncovered information that led them to suspect the Turner Drysdale referred to is Turner Carson, who has been linked to other robberies in the past. The SP sent over the photo I showed you in the hope of tracking down Carson for questioning. I suspect he's still on the island, although if he is, he's lying low. So far we haven't been able to fish him out. I have a plan, but it involves you and could be dangerous."

Tanner looked at Finn with determination in his eyes. "How can I help?"

If Carson was still on the island it made no sense that he hadn't hunted down Tanner and finished what Drysdale interrupted unless he either didn't know how to find him or he'd heard he'd lost his memory and figured he didn't pose a threat. Finn didn't know for certain that Carson was still on the island, but several of the people he'd interviewed in the past few days claimed to have seen him. It made no sense that the guy would still be hanging around unless Drysdale had hidden the money they'd stolen somewhere on the island and Carson still hadn't found it. Of course if that were true Carson was an idiot for killing Drysdale before he recovered the money, but Finn had learned that he wasn't known for being the brightest tool in the shed.

Finn's plan was to use Tanner to flush out Carson. It seemed to me to be too dangerous, but Finn assured me he'd have eyes on Tanner the entire time. Finn had arranged for backup deputies to join him in the sting, which would begin at the scene of the crime. The undercover deputies, dressed like bar patrons, were already in place when Tanner showed up at the bar that evening. He'd been told to act like he was drunk as a skunk and then proceed to spout off quite loudly that he knew who had killed the man whose body had been found on the north shore and had proof to back it up. Once word was out that Tanner planned to take his proof to the sheriff unless Carson paid him a large amount of money, Tanner sat at the bar pretending to drink shots while Finn and his men sat back and waited for Carson to show up.

"I really, really hate this," I complained to Cody, Tara, and Siobhan. Finn had insisted that we wait in my cabin until everything was over.

"I'm not the brave sort and I don't want to get shot, but it doesn't seem right that we're just sitting here while Tanner risks his life," Tara added.

"Finn knows what he's doing," Siobhan insisted. "If he says Tanner is safe then he is."

"Do you think this is going to work?" Tara asked. "It seems like this Carson guy would have to be pretty dumb to fall for such an obvious setup."

"I checked the guy out," Cody informed us. "He's known for being rash and impulsive."

Tara went into the kitchen to stress cook while Siobhan poured herself a glass of wine and Cody went upstairs to return a few phone calls. I decided pacing was my drug of choice, but my cabin is small and the amount of space I had for that activity wasn't really adequate.

"I'm going to take Max out," I announced.

"Finn said to stay in the cabin," Siobhan reminded me.

"I know. I'm just going to be right out front. It's been a few hours since Max has been out and he has that look about him."

"Okay, but stay close," Siobhan warned me.

Max chased the waves as I paced back and forth in front of the cabin. I looked out toward the dark horizon and wondered where the day had gone. The interview with Tanner had taken place at noon and now it was completely dark. If I had to account for the hours in between I wasn't sure I'd be able to.

I followed Max as he chased something only he could see. It was a quiet, peaceful evening and I felt much of the stress I'd been carrying around drain from my body as I drifted farther and farther away from the cabin. Don't get me wrong; I didn't venture far. The lights from the kitchen were still bright and I could see Cody standing in front of the window upstairs. I was about to call Max back and head inside when I noticed the headlights of an approaching car turn off the main highway onto the peninsula road. Maybe it was Finn. Maybe this whole thing was over.

I turned back around and looked for Max but didn't see him.

"Max," I called.

I heard him bark and looked in that direction. He'd wandered farther down the beach than I'd realized.

"Come on back. It's time for dinner."

I noticed the car's headlights turn into the drive I shared with Aunt Maggie, who lived in the big house just behind my cabin. My chest filled with anticipation as I waited for Max to make his way back down the beach. As soon as he'd caught up with me I turned and headed home. I'd almost reached the cabin when I noticed that Clarence was coming toward me down the beach.

"What are you doing out here?"

"Meow."

I don't claim to speak cat, but it was obvious something was wrong.

"It's the car. It isn't Finn, is it?"

"Meow."

I quietly crept toward the trees that grew to the left of the property. If there was danger at the cabin, approaching from the beach would make me a sitting duck. I made my way around to the back, where I could peek in a side window. I gasped when I saw Cody, Siobhan, and Tara all sitting on the sofa while a man stood in front of them holding a gun. As quietly as I could, I slipped back into the woods and called Finn. Of course he told me to hang tight until he arrived, but with my sister, my best friend, and my boyfriend in trouble, hanging tight wasn't something I was able to do.

"We need a plan," I whispered to Clarence. He hadn't done much of anything since that very first day he'd arrived, but the fact that he was still with me indicated that his job wasn't done. To my way of thinking, helping me save the others would make a good reason to have stayed.

"Meow."

"Yes, I know waiting for Finn is the plan, but it wouldn't hurt to at least brainstorm a plan B. What if the guy in the cabin has an accomplice in the bar? If the guy with the gun gets wind that half the patrons in the bar have suddenly gotten up and left he's going to figure out that the cops know what he's up to. The last thing we need is for the cops to storm in and create a hostage situation."

"Meow."

"I know Finn is smart and I know I should trust him. I do trust him. Let's at least see if we can get closer to see what's going on."

I crept as quietly as I could to the kitchen window. It was over the sink and small, allowing only a limited view of the interior of the cabin, but I was afraid if I tried to peek into one of the larger windows the man with the gun would see me.

They all seemed to be in some sort of a holding pattern. The man with the gun was pacing back and forth, looking more than a little stressed. After a few minutes he told Cody and Tara to sit on the chairs in the dining area. Then he instructed Siobhan to tie them up with rope I assume he'd brought with him.

Once Tara and Cody were tied up he grabbed Siobhan by the hair and motioned to the side door. I commanded Max to stay as Clarence ran to the car. I followed behind and opened the back door, and we slid into the backseat. We closed the door and lay as flat as we could on the floor. It was dark, so I hoped the man wouldn't notice us.

"Get in," he instructed Siobhan just seconds after Clarence and I were settled.

"What are you going to do with me?" my sister asked. Fear was evident in her voice as she slid onto the front passenger seat.

"You're going to call your boyfriend and work out a trade. I'll let you go if he turns the scumbag who's threatening me over to me."

"He'll never do that."

"He will if he wants to see his pretty lady alive again."

I held my breath as Siobhan called Finn and relayed the message the man had given her. Of course neither of them knew I'd already called Finn and he knew exactly what was going on.

"He wants to meet," Siobhan told the man with the gun. "He needs to know where."

"Tell him to tie the man from the bar to one of the trees near the front of the grove off Bloomingdale Road. Once he's done that he's to head over to Harthaven Market, where he's to take a selfie of himself in front of the sign. I'll be watching from a distance to make sure there's no funny business going on. When I'm sure there are no cops in the area I'll retrieve my prize and leave the pretty lady in his place."

Siobhan shared the information the gunman had given her. Then he grabbed the phone and tossed it out the window. "Can't have them tracking us, now can we?"

As it turned out, Turner Carson wasn't the idiot everyone had assumed. He drove to the top of the bluff overlooking the orchard and waited. He could see everything that was going on below, but he was far enough away that the state police, if there were any, wouldn't be able to nab him.

I knew I had to think and I had to think fast. If Finn did as Carson asked and took Tanner to the grove there would be nothing to stop him from shooting him and then turning and shooting Siobhan as well. We were on an island, though, so there weren't a lot of places to run. The only thing that made sense was that Carson had a boat waiting to take him away.

I needed a plan. Clarence crawled under the seat. I was afraid he was going to come out on the other end and Carson would see him, so I reached in to pull him back. My hand met with metal. It felt like a tire iron. I slowly wrapped my hand around the instrument and pulled it back toward me.

"What are you doing over there?" Carson demanded.

"Nothing. Really. I'm just sitting here," Siobhan insisted. "I guess I am a little fidgety. Maybe my foot hit the door panel."

"Well, sit quieter. I hear rustling and it's disturbing my concentration."

Despite what she'd said, Siobhan had been sitting perfectly still, and I realized the rustling Carter had heard was me.

"It looks like your boyfriend has arrived at the orchard. Now we just need to confirm he's alone."

"Can you see them through those binoculars?" Siobhan asked. "It's so dark."

"I can see them."

"Please don't kill Tanner or Finn, and please don't kill me. I'm sure we can work something out. We can get you money, a boat, anything you want."

"Quiet down. I need to focus."

Once I had the tire iron firmly in hand I motioned for Clarence to create a diversion. I just hoped the cat wouldn't get shot for his efforts. It sounded like Carson was looking through binoculars, which could mean he'd set his gun down. It was probably in his lap.

Everything happened so fast. Clarence jumped up onto the backseat and then onto the back of the front before pouncing on Carter's head. Carter threw his hands in the air to dislodge the cat and I sat up and hit him in the head as hard as I could with the tire iron. Somehow Siobhan managed to grab the gun.

Carter was out cold, but Siobhan pointed the gun at him just in case.

"God, Cait. I thought I was going to die while I waited for you to make your move."

"You knew I was in here?"

"I could smell the peaches."

"I'm going to hug you so hard in a few minutes," I promised my sister, "but first I'm going to call Finn to tell him to get over here and pick up his package."

Chapter 13

Saturday, December 24

"Did you see where Cody went?" I asked Tara.

"He and Finn went to find more chairs. It seems word of Mr. Parsons's Christmas Eve party has made the rounds and there are quite a few more guests then we expected."

I opened the oven to baste one of the four turkeys we were baking. "That's okay. We have a ton of food. As soon as Mom got together with Francine the menu went from simple to extravagant."

"I noticed Danny brought Tawny," Tara commented while peeling potatoes.

I stopped what I was doing and looked at my best friend. She and Danny had shared an on-again, off-again relationship of sorts and I wasn't 100 percent sure she was over him. "Are you okay with that?"

"More than okay," Tara assured me. "I really like Tawny. She's a hard worker and I think she'll make a good addition to our staff, especially now that the part-time help we hired last summer has moved on to other things."

"She does seem to be a natural with the customers," I agreed.

"She's sweet and sincere and I think she's going to work out. And I'm happy she has Danny looking out for her. It's early to tell where their friendship may end up, but he seems to be genuinely concerned about her comfort and welfare. He was never quite so charming when we dated."

I began assembling the ingredients we'd need for the candied yams. "Danny has his moments. He can be charming if motivated to do so, but he can be sort of self-centered as well. He doesn't seem the kind to know what to do with a baby, so I can't help but wonder if his friendship with Tawny will last once the baby is born."

"I think Danny might surprise you," Tara insisted. "Of course he won't be as good with kids as Tanner. That man really does have a knack."

"Speaking of Tanner, how's he doing now that he's regained all his memory?"

"He's doing okay," Tara answered. "He's sad to be missing Christmas with Hannah, but he's happy to have a new start to look forward to."

Tanner had spoken to his brother-in-law, who not only had agreed not to foreclose on the bookstore but also agreed to find another building on the island where Tanner could open a restaurant.

"He told me that as long as he stays sober, Anthony is going to encourage his sister to let Hannah come to the island to visit him one weekend a month," Tara added.

"Do you think he can stay sober?" I asked.

Tara looked up from the pile of potatoes she was working on. "I do. He called around and found a local AA meeting. He has plans to start next week. Anthony has agreed to get him set up in a house, so the two of us are going house hunting on Monday. I think Tanner is a good guy who found himself in a difficult situation and acted in a less than productive way. He's made me a couple of meals, so I can attest to the fact that he knows how to cook. I think he'll do very well once he gets settled. Did you remember the cheese for the broccoli?"

"It's on the top shelf of the refrigerator."

Tara opened the refrigerator and stuck her head in. "Who brought the cheesecake?"

"Mom. It's my favorite. I wasn't sure how she was going to do with Christmas this year after everything that's happened, but she seems to be enjoying herself now that the holiday is actually here."

"I was chatting with Aiden, who said he's going to help your mom look for a house she can afford that has a larger space for entertaining."

"Mom does love to gather all her chicks together and the kitchen in the condo really isn't big enough."

"Seems like everyone is going to be house hunting after the holiday," Tara commented. "I'm going to help Tanner find both a house and a building to use for a restaurant, Danny mentioned helping Tawny find a place better suited for raising a child, Aiden is going to help your mom find a house with a larger living area, and Siobhan told me that she and Finn were going to look for a house to live in after they get married."

"Finn's place is pretty small and Siobhan mentioned wanting to start a family right away. I wouldn't be at all surprised if she's pregnant by next Christmas."

"Have they set a date?" Tara asked.

"I think they decided on May. She doesn't want to commit to which Saturday in the month until she has a chance to look for a venue."

"Makes sense."

"I think we've done what we can here until the turkeys are ready to come out. I'm going to find Cody to see if he needs any help, if that's okay with you."

"Not a problem. Tanner should be back from the store any minute and he can help me finish up here. You've already done so much to make this party happen. Go, relax, and mingle with your guests."

I texted Cody to ask him where he was. He was at Francine's, picking up her folding chairs. Then he planned to head over to Maggie's to get hers as well. I decided to walk down the beach to meet him at Maggie's. It had been hot in the kitchen and the fresh air felt wonderful. I was halfway down the beach when I ran into Clarence. I stopped and picked him up.

"What are you doing out here?"

"Meow."

"Were you looking for me?"

Clarence began to purr.

"Do you need me to take you some place?"

"Meow."

One of the things I'd learned from working with Tansy's cats was that they were never mine to keep. When they were done with their tasks some found their way back to their original home, while others moved on to new ones.

"Let's go find Cody. We'll take you wherever you want to go together."

I texted Tara and told her what we were doing. She texted back and said both Mom and Francine had joined her in the kitchen and Tanner was back as well, so she had plenty of help. She estimated that dinner would be ready in a couple of hours. Guests were still arriving and Mr. Parsons had everyone gathered in the ballroom for drinks, appetizers, and small talk.

When I explained to Cody and Finn what I intended to do, Finn offered to take the chairs they had gathered back to the party so Cody could go with Max and me to take Clarence wherever he wanted to go.

"It's crazy the way you can communicate with these cats," Cody said as Clarence let me know in which direction we should drive and I passed the route to Cody.

"You're right, it is sort of crazy. But it works, and I think I'm settling into my role. Take a left at the next intersection."

Cody did as I instructed. Eventually, Clarence had us stop at a small house at the end of a dirt drive. The house didn't have any exterior lights, making it seem almost deserted. I got out of the car and Clarence followed me. I knocked on the door, which was opened by an elderly woman wearing an old house dress.

"Can I help you?"

I glanced down at Clarence. "I may have found your cat."

The woman looked confused. "My cat? I don't have a cat."

I wasn't sure what to say. I could see the woman was alone. The television was on and there was a microwave meal on a TV tray. I figured the next move was up to Clarence, so I waited. He meowed and the woman opened the door just a crack. Clarence trotted inside.

"This is Clarence," I said as the cat wound his way around the woman's legs. "He wanted to come here tonight. I'm not sure why, but he was quite insistent. I thought maybe this was his home. Does anyone else live here?"

"No, it's just me. I've lived alone since my husband died a few months ago. You say his name is Clarence?"

"Yes, ma'am."

The woman bent down and picked up the cat, who began to purr. I noticed a tear slip down the woman's cheek. "My husband's name was Clarence." She held the cat to her chest as tears streamed down her face. "I don't know who you are or how you came to be on my doorstep tonight, but I want you to know you've just given this old woman without a hope of finding happiness her one and only Christmas wish."

"Christmas wish?"

"My husband had been sick before he passed. He knew he didn't have a lot of time, but before he died he promised to send me a Christmas miracle to let me know he wasn't gone from my life but would be watching over me until it was time for us to be together again."

Recipes from Kathi

Herb and Bacon Cheeseball
Chicken Artichoke Dip
Beefy Nachos
Steak and Baked Potato Soup

Recipes from Readers

Christmas Ribbon Gelatin Salad—submitted by Nancy Farris

Versatile Cranberry Nut Bread with Optional Glaze—submitted by Joanne Kocourek

Orange Creamsicle Fudge—submitted by Elizabeth Dent

Chocolate Chip Cream Cheese Bars—submitted by Lisa Millett

Ice Box Cookies—submitted by Pam Curran

Karen's Pumpkin, Black Bean, and Bacon Soup—submitted by Karen Owen

Christmas Cheeseball—submitted by Linda Mierka

Turkey Cheese Baked Soup—submitted by Marie Rice

Herb and Bacon Cheese Ball

12 oz. cream cheese, softened
6 pieces bacon, cooked crisp and crumbled
1 can (4 oz.) diced green chilies
1 tbs. chopped garlic
1 tbs. chopped fresh basil
1 tbs. chopped chives
1 cup grated Parmesan cheese
1 cup grated Jack cheese
1 cup grated cheddar cheese
2 tsp. horseradish
⅔ cup chopped almonds

Mix all ingredients except almonds in a bowl. I just use my hands to mix everything together. Form a ball. Lay almonds on a breadboard. Roll cheese ball in almonds until coated.

Wrap in plastic wrap and chill overnight. Serve with crackers.

Chicken Artichoke Dip

Combine in large bowl:

2 large chicken breasts, cooked and cubed
2 cups artichoke hearts, chopped
8 oz. cream cheese, softened
I cup grated Parmesan cheese
1 cup Pepper Jack cheese, grated
1 cup cheddar cheese, grated
14 oz. diced green chiles (Ortega)
1 cup mayonnaise
Salt and pepper to taste

Pour into 9 x 13 pan. Top with additional grated cheese (as much as you want).

Bake at 350 degrees until bubbly (about 45 minutes).

Serve with chips, crackers, French bread slices, or tortillas.

Beefy Nachos

Make meat the day before your gathering.

Trim all fat off boneless rib roast (size depends on amount of meat desired). Season with salt, pepper, and garlic powder. Place in slow cooker. Cover meat with store-bought salsa, either hot or mild, depending on preference.

Cook on high until meat begins to pull apart. Continue to shred meat as it cooks. When it's completely done (cooking time depends on amount of meat and heat of slow cooker, but about 8 hours), spoon meat from sauce with slotted spoon.

Refrigerate.

Next day:

Layer tortilla chips on cookie sheet. Cover with grated cheese; I use sharp cheddar and Jack, but you can use whatever.

Place cookie sheet under broiler with heat set on low.

Reheat the meat on stove or in microwave. When cheese is melted on tortilla chips cover with meat—be sure it's drained of excess fluid—and serve with sour cream, guacamole, diced tomatoes, or whatever you'd like to add.

Steak and Baked Potato Soup

1 lb. beef tenderloin cut into small pieces
1 cup chopped onion
1 tsp. salt
4 cups cubed potatoes (can use cubed hash browns)
4 cups beef broth
1 cup steak sauce (mild or spicy)
2 tsp. chili powder
1 tsp. cayenne pepper

Garnish:

1 carton sour cream
1 cup cheddar cheese, grated
1 cup bacon, fried and crumbled

In large pan sauté beef, onion, and salt in oil until steak is cooked through.

Stir in potatoes, broth, steak sauce, and spices.

Bring to a boil. Reduce heat and simmer until potatoes are tender.

Spoon into serving bowls and garnish with sour cream, cheese, and bacon pieces.

Christmas Ribbon Gelatin Salad

Submitted by Nancy Farris

At the holidays, my mother always served a gelatin salad with the meal on a fancy little side plate on top of a piece of ruffled lettuce. No green salad at a holiday meal for us! Here is her holiday gelatin salad for you to enjoy. It does take some time to make (the layers have to set up before you go to the next layer), but it was the holidays after all!

Bottom layer:
1 3-oz. pkg. lime gelatin
1 cup boiling water
¾ cup cold water

Empty gelatin into a bowl. Add boiling water and stir until dissolved. Add ¾ cup cold water and stir well. Pour into a 2 x 9 x 13 pan that's been lightly sprayed with cooking spray. Refrigerate until set, 1–2 hours.

Middle layer:
1 3-oz. pkg. lemon gelatin
1 cup boiling water
½ cup minimarshmallows
8 oz. cream cheese, cut in cubes and softened

to room temperature
8 oz. crushed pineapple, drained
1 cup whipping cream
¼ cup chopped pecans (optional)

Empty gelatin into bowl. Stir in boiling water and stir until dissolved. Stir in the minimarshmallows and set aside for a few minutes so they will begin to melt a little. Add cream cheese and beat until blended. Stir in the crushed pineapple, whipping cream, and pecans. Chill until thickened, then spread over green layer. Chill until firm, about 1 hour.

Top layer:
1 3-oz. pkg. cherry Jell-O
1 cup boiling water
¾ cup cold water

Empty Jell-O in bowl. Add boiling water and stir until dissolved. Add ¾ cup cold water and stir well. Set aside until it's at room temperature and spread over the middle layer.

It's best to refrigerate overnight. Cut into squares and serve on a fancy salad plate and top with a dollop of whipped cream.

Number of servings depend on how big the squares are. Mom sometimes made it in an 8 x 8 dish so it would be thicker.

Versatile Cranberry Nut Bread with Optional Glaze

Submitted by Joanne Kocourek

I was looking for something I could make with the extra cans of whole berry cranberry sauce (and jellied cranberry sauce) that wasn't used at Thanksgiving. I wanted a bread that tasted great and was easy to make. Even our granddaughter, who doesn't like cranberries, devoured it!

2 cups flour
2 tsp. baking powder
1 tsp. cinnamon
½ tsp. nutmeg
½ tsp. salt
½ cup butter, softened
½ cup sugar
1 tsp. vanilla
1 egg
1 14-oz. can whole berry cranberry sauce
¼ cup orange marmalade or 1 tbs. orange zest (optional)
1 cup chopped walnuts (optional)

Preheat oven to 350 degrees. Grease a 2½ x 4½ x 8½-inch loaf pan.

Combine flour, baking powder, cinnamon, nutmeg, and salt in a small mixing bowl; set aside.

Using an electric mixer beat butter with sugar in a medium mixing bowl until light and fluffy. Add vanilla and egg; mix well. Break up cranberry sauce with a fork and add to the butter mixture. Add orange marmalade or orange zest and nuts (these are all optional). Add dry ingredients to the cranberry mixture, mixing just until the dry ingredients are moist.

Spread batter evenly into prepared loaf pan. Bake until golden brown and a toothpick inserted into the center comes out clean, about 1 hour and 15 minutes. If bread begins to brown too quickly, loosely cover with foil and continue to bake until bread tests done.

Note: The batter can also be divided into two small loaf pans or four mini loaf pans. For smaller loaves the baking time does need to be adjusted. The small loaves make nice gifts.

Optional White Chocolate Cranberry Glaze

Melt ⅓ cup white chocolate chips into ⅓ cup jellied cranberry sauce. Add 1 tsp. butter, ¼ tsp. lemon extract, and 2 tbs. light corn syrup. While the loaf of bread is still warm top with the glaze.

Orange Creamsicle Fudge

Submitted by Elizabeth Dent

We found this recipe and I make it at Christmastime when the kids and their families come on Christmas Eve. If I don't have it, they all want to know where it is.

Orange Creamsicle Fudge features swirls of sweet white chocolate fudge mixed with bright, fragrant orange-flavored fudge. Be sure to taste the orange fudge before pouring it into the pan and adjust the amount of flavoring to suit your taste, because the potency of different orange extracts can vary greatly.

2 cups granulated sugar
¾ cup heavy cream
6 oz. (1.5 sticks) butter
1 pkg. (12-oz.) white chocolate chips
1 jar (7 oz.) marshmallow cream (or fluff)
1 tbs. orange extract
orange (or a combination of red and yellow) food coloring

Prepare a 9 x 13 pan by lining it with aluminum foil and spraying the foil with nonstick cooking spray.

In a large, heavy saucepan combine the sugar, cream, and butter over medium heat. Continually stir the mixture until the butter melts and the sugar dissolves. Brush down the sides with a wet pastry brush.

Bring the mixture to a boil, and once it starts boiling insert a candy thermometer. Cook the candy until it reaches 240 degrees on the thermometer, which should take about 4–5 minutes.

After the candy reaches 240 degrees remove the pan from the heat and immediately stir in the white chocolate chips and marshmallow cream. Stir until the white chocolate has melted and the fudge is completely smooth.

Working quickly, pour about a third of the white fudge into a bowl and set aside. To the remaining fudge add the orange extract and orange food coloring, stirring until it is a smooth, even color. It is important to perform these steps quickly, because the fudge will start to set if you take too long and the end result won't be smooth.

Pour the orange fudge into the prepared pan and spread it into an even layer. Drop the white fudge over the top by the spoonful, then drag a table knife or toothpick through the fudge to create orange-white swirls. You can spray your hands with nonstick cooking spray and gently press them into the top to smooth out the swirls if desired.

Allow the fudge to set at room temperature for 2 hours, or in the refrigerator for 1 hour. To cut, pull the fudge out of the pan using the foil as handles. Use a large sharp knife to cut the fudge into small, 1-inch squares. Store Orange Creamsicle Fudge in an airtight container in the refrigerator for up to a week and bring it to room temperature to serve.

Note: We added zest of one orange. Also did the drop test in water...should start to form soft ball. The broil time may vary!

Chocolate Chip Cream Cheese Bars

Submitted by Lisa Millett

My roommate in college, Deena, gave me this recipe freshman year 1981. Her mother, who was from Italy, used to make these bars all the time. I began to make them for Christmas that year and have continued every year since then. The year after we graduated, her mom got sick and passed away really quickly. I felt and still feel honored to have a legacy from her mom, who was a sweetheart. My husband also loved these delicious bars, which are simple to make but combine your chocolate chip goodness with a cheesecakelike center and are hard to resist. When my husband developed a swallowing disorder and got to the point of needing a feeding tube to survive, he would still ask me to make the bars. He wasn't able to eat them anymore, but he enjoyed seeing and smelling them, which broke my heart. He passed away three years ago from stomach cancer, but I still think of him and my roommate's mom when I make them. It makes me still have a part of them here with me.

2 large rolls of chocolate chip cookie dough
2 pkg. cream cheese
1 tsp. vanilla
¾ cup sugar
2 eggs
wax paper

Preheat oven to 350 degrees. Grease 9 x 13 baking dish with PAM spray. Flatten first cookie dough roll on bottom of glass dish.

Blend cream cheese, vanilla, sugar, and eggs in separate dish with electric mixer. Spread this mix on top of cookie dough in glass dish.

Use piece of wax paper about 18 inches long to roll out other cookie dough onto. Try to make it even with glass dish dimensions. Flip wax paper with cookie dough over onto top of glass dish. Remove wax paper. Even out dough on top of dish if needed.

Bake at 350 degrees for 45 minutes. Take out and let cool, then refrigerate for 2 hours. Take out and cut into brownie-size pieces.

Best served cold.

Ice Box Cookies

Submitted by Pam Curran

This cookie recipe came from my mother. It was one of seven or eight she made at Christmas when we were younger. Right after Thanksgiving, the baking and freezing of cookies began. We always looked forward to having these at Christmas. Of course, we did get a sample cookie sometimes.

1 lb. butter or margarine
1½ cups light brown sugar
1½ cups regular sugar
3 eggs, beaten stiff
6 cups flour
1 tsp. soda
2 tsp. cinnamon
Juice of 1 lemon
1 cup pecans

Cream butter or margarine together with sugars. Add beaten eggs. Mix well. Add flour, soda, and cinnamon, sifted together. Add lemon juice and pecans. Mix and put on wax paper after shaping into 3 rolls. Chill in ice box (refrigerator) overnight. Slice about ¼ inch and bake in a 350-degree oven until light brown, 8–9 minutes.

Karen's Pumpkin, Black Bean, and Bacon Soup

Submitted by Karen Owen

4–6 pieces bacon, rough chopped
1 medium onion, chopped
1tbs. minced garlic
1 14-oz. can pumpkin (not pumpkin pie filling)
4 cups chicken stock
1 14-oz. can black beans, drained and rinsed
1½ tsp. Cajun Seasoning Mix
Salt and pepper to taste

Heat a cast-iron fry pan over medium heat and add chopped bacon, rendering it slowly until crisp; remove the bacon from the pan and drain, reserve the drippings.

Add onion to the pan and 1 tbs. of the drippings; sauté until onion is translucent. Add garlic and continue cooking for 1 minute.

In a Dutch oven or large soup pot place pumpkin and chicken stock. Wisk them together and bring them up to a simmer, add onions, bacon, and black beans. Add seasoning, stir, and bring up to a boil. Taste and adjust seasoning if you would like. If you find it too flavorful add some sour cream; if not add more seasoning.

Serve with corn bread, a cup of tea, and a fall-themed cozy mystery.

Christmas Cheeseball

Submitted by Linda Mierka

1 jar or pkg. chipped beef
6 green onions, diced greens included
1 small can crushed pineapple
1 8-oz. pkg. cream cheese
¼ tsp. onion powder

Mix all ingredients together and serve with assorted crackers.

You can also shape into a ball and roll in minced walnuts or pecans.

Turkey Cheese Baked Soup

Submitted by Marie Rice

1 large white onion, finely chopped
2 lbs. cooked turkey meat
1 26-oz. can cream of chicken condensed soup
1 32-oz. carton low-sodium chicken or
vegetable broth
½ tsp. black pepper
Dash or two of cayenne pepper
Dash or two of garlic powder (optional)
8 cups shredded cheddar cheese
Milled flax seed (optional)

Sauté chopped onion in a 4-quart pot until
cooked. Chop turkey meat into bite-sized
pieces and add to pot, along with all remaining
ingredients except cheese and flax seed.
Warm over medium-high heat, stirring. Adjust
seasonings as needed. Let cook for about 6
minutes once warmed up.

Preheat oven to 350 degrees.

Spray or butter a deep 9 x 13 casserole dish
or an 11 x 15 oversize casserole baking dish.
Ladle ⅔ of the turkey sauce into the casserole
dish. Spread about ⅔ of the cheese over the
sauce. Layer the remainder of the turkey
sauce and then the remainder of the cheese.

Add an optional sprinkling of milled flax seed over the final cheese layer for a little crunch in the topping.

Bake for about 35 minutes. Allow to cool 10–15 minutes before serving.

Notes:
* I frequently put a 3-lb. turkey breast roast into a slow cooker throughout the year. Depending on how quickly our family goes through the turkey meat, sometimes I can get one of these soups cooked.
* Leftover turkey from Thanksgiving or Christmas are perfect to use in this recipe.
* Use any combination of white and/or dark turkey meat.
* Chopped onion can be placed into the 4-quart pot without sautéing it, but the sauté action gives it greater flavor.
* I find soup mugs to be the best way to serve this soup versus a soup/cereal bowl because you can warm your hands on a soup mug ~smile~.

Books by Kathi Daley

Come for the murder, stay for the romance.

Zoe Donovan Cozy Mystery:

Halloween Hijinks
The Trouble With Turkeys
Christmas Crazy
Cupid's Curse
Big Bunny Bump-off
Beach Blanket Barbie
Maui Madness
Derby Divas
Haunted Hamlet
Turkeys, Tuxes, and Tabbies
Christmas Cozy
Alaskan Alliance
Matrimony Meltdown
Soul Surrender
Heavenly Honeymoon
Hopscotch Homicide
Ghostly Graveyard
Santa Sleuth
Shamrock Shenanigans
Kitten Kaboodle
Costume Catastrophe
Candy Cane Caper
Holiday Hangover – *January 2017*

Zimmerman Academy The New Normal

Ashton Falls Cozy Cookbook

Tj Jensen Paradise Lake Mysteries by Henery Press
Pumpkins in Paradise
Snowmen in Paradise
Bikinis in Paradise
Christmas in Paradise
Puppies in Paradise
Halloween in Paradise
Treasure in Paradise – *April 2017*

Whales and Tails Cozy Mystery:
Romeow and Juliet
The Mad Catter
Grimm's Furry Tail
Much Ado About Felines
Legend of Tabby Hollow
The Cat of Christmas Past
A Tale of Two Tabbies
The Great Catsby
Count Catula
The Cat of Christmas Present

Seacliff High Mystery:

The Secret
The Curse
The Relic
The Conspiracy
The Grudge

Sand and Sea Hawaiian Mystery:

Murder at Dolphin Bay
Murder at Sunrise Beach
Murder at the Witching Hour
Murder at Christmas – *December 2016*

Road to Christmas Romance:

Road to Christmas Past

Kathi Daley lives with her husband, kids, grandkids, and Bernese mountain dogs in beautiful Lake Tahoe. When she isn't writing, she likes to read (preferably at the beach or by the fire), cook (preferably something with chocolate or cheese), and garden (planting and planning, not weeding). She also enjoys spending time on the water when she's not hiking, biking, or snowshoeing the miles of desolate trails surrounding her home.

Kathi uses the mountain setting in which she lives, along with the animals (wild and domestic) that share her home, as inspiration for her cozy mysteries.

Kathi is a top 100 mystery writer for Amazon and she won the 2014 award for both Best Cozy Mystery Author and Best Cozy Mystery Series.

She currently writes five series: Zoe Donovan Cozy Mysteries, Whales and Tails Island Mysteries, Sand and Sea Hawaiian Mysteries, Tj Jensen Paradise Lake Mysteries, and Seacliff High Teen Mysteries.

Giveaway:

I do a giveaway for books, swag, and gift cards every week in my newsletter, *The Daley Weekly*
http://eepurl.com/NRPDf

Other links to check out:
Kathi Daley Blog – publishes each Friday
http://kathidaleyblog.com
Webpage – www.kathidaley.com
Facebook at Kathi Daley Books –
www.facebook.com/kathidaleybooks
Kathi Daley Teen –
www.facebook.com/kathidaleyteen
Kathi Daley Books Group Page –
https://www.facebook.com/groups/569578823146850/
E-mail – kathidaley@kathidaley.com
Goodreads –
https://www.goodreads.com/author/show/7278377.Kathi_Daley
Twitter at Kathi Daley@kathidaley –
https://twitter.com/kathidaley
Amazon Author Page –
https://www.amazon.com/author/kathidaley

BookBub –
https://www.bookbub.com/authors/kathi-daley
Pinterest –
http://www.pinterest.com/kathidaley/

Made in the USA
Middletown, DE
30 December 2017